SURVIVING HER CHRISTMAS PRESENT

SURVIVING HER CHRISTMAS PRESENT

KYLEIGH McCLOUD

Copyright © Kyleigh McCloud 2021

All rights reserved. No part of this publication may be reproduced, stored in a retrieval system, or transmitted, in any form or by any means, electronic, mechanical, photocopying, recording or otherwise, without the prior written permission from the author. For permission requests, contact Kyleigh McCloud at kyleighmccloud.author@gmail.com.

This is a work of fiction. Names, characters, businesses, places, events, locales, and incidents are either the products of the author's imagination or used in a fictitious manner. Any resemblance to actual persons, living or dead, or actual events is purely coincidental.

Available in e-book and print.

Print ISBN: 978-1-7357192-2-1

Ebook ISBN: 978-1-7357192-3-8

First Edition: 2021

Editor: Dennis Doty

Cover designer: Sydney Blackburn

Book Formatter: KH Formatting

For more information, please visit my website:
kyleighmccloud.com

Also by
Kyleigh McCloud

Her Mother's Last Christmas Gift
Warrior's Imprisonment in Phobia!: An Anthology of Fear
Three Colors of Life in Kaleidoscope

For a complete list check out kyleighmccloud.com.

A Note from the Author

When writing Surviving Her Christmas Present, I struggled with deciding what kind of domestic abuse and how much detail should be included. Domestic abuse is ugly. I settled upon writing the ugly truth of emotional, physical, and sexual abuse. Too many people suffer in silence, and I hope Mary's story with domestic violence will bring awareness. If you or someone you know are enduring domestic abuse, please seek help immediately.

I'm dedicating this book to all those who survived domestic violence and to those who are currently surviving in an abusive relationship.

One

I pulled my coat tighter. Though the temperature was thirty degrees and sunny, the chill within refused to remove its clutch. Jake would have beaten her with that belt. I shivered. If I hadn't intervened, the doctor would have gotten another made-up excuse.

"Huwwy up," Serenity chided.

The library lay beyond the street, our haven three blocks from home. They hadn't decorated yet. Faint Christmas music carried from the speakers in downtown Spruce Point. Maybe the city workers would start decorating the library after finishing downtown.

We jogged across the street, and Serenity leapt over the curb in a fit of giggles. "I did it."

I ruffled her hat. "Good job, sweetie."

"Mary," Jake shouted in the distance. "Come back! I'm sorry."

"That's Daddy."

I herded Serenity up the steps, and we entered the building's entryway. We weren't coming back until he slept it off.

In the library, a coffee pot gurgled. The fresh brewed aroma permeated throughout our sanctuary and loosened the stiffness into a homey environment. Serenity ran to a child-sized coat rack, her boots clunking across the floor. She traced the hook.

"Good morning," an elderly woman with salt-and-pepper curls said to Serenity. "Would you like help with taking off your coat?"

"I do it."

Serenity jerked the zipper down and snagged it at the bottom of her jacket. She tugged at the zipper. When the zipper refused to budge, my daughter lifted the jammed portion and whined, "I can't get it."

"Let me see." The librarian pulled out a small chair and sat in it. Bony fingers wriggled the fabric of my daughter's coat. The elderly woman glided the zipper down until the jacket parted. "There you go."

"Tank you." Serenity hung the jacket in the cubby then ran to a toy box. She squealed, "New toys!"

One by one, building blocks announced their presence with a thud. Serenity continued pulling out more.

"Serenity, honey, remember we talked about being quiet in the library?"

"Oh, she's fine." The librarian collected yesterday's newspaper off an end table and replaced it with today's. A smile emerged. "Children are meant to be heard."

Serenity yanked neatly stacked jigsaw puzzles from a nearby shelf and dumped the pieces onto the floor. She took multiple pieces and jammed them into the puzzle. When she couldn't fit the pieces in the correct slots, they soon joined the blocks on the floor.

"Excuse me. Can I have yesterday's paper, please?" I asked.

"Today's paper is out, if you want that."

Serenity pulled a book off the shelf, opened it, and read her own made-up story out loud.

"Please… I need to find a job."

My daughter tossed the book, and it landed on the pile of blocks and puzzles. She took another.

I marched over to Serenity and snatched the book from her hand. "We're leaving. Go get your coat."

"Why?" Serenity flattened her lips. She crossed her arms and narrowed her eyes into slits while glaring.

I gathered the scattered blocks and puzzle pieces. "You're being too noisy."

Serenity stomped to the coat rack and tugged her coat off the hook, muttering while jamming her arms into its sleeves. As she tried to zip her jacket, the zipper snagged once again. Rather than ask for help, Serenity pouted by the door.

I finished collecting the rest of her mess and added them into the toy box. The tossed book still lay on the floor. I scooped up the overturned book and studied its pages for damage. "Sorry for the mess she made."

The librarian extended the newspaper. "Here's yesterday's paper. Good luck on the job hunt."

"Thanks." I traded the book for her newspaper and apologized once again.

At the door, I freed Serenity's zipper. After I helped her push open the door, I folded the newspaper and tucked it inside my pocket. We couldn't go home yet.

I brushed the crusted snow off the park bench and settled into a comfortable position while Serenity dashed toward the playground equipment. The sun provided enough warmth on this balmy December day, a blessing for this morning. A smile burst through as my daughter climbed the platforms to the slide.

"Mommy. Mommy, watch me," Serenity shouted in a shrill voice. She towered above the slide and raised her arms over her head.

A gasp caught in my throat.

My little gymnast somersaulted down the slide and landed in a snow mound with a shriek. She stood unharmed. A grin shone on her face at the accomplishment.

I released the breath I had been holding. We couldn't afford another trip to the emergency room. The excuses became more difficult for the staff to believe with each hospital visit. They suspected.

Serenity loped toward me with open arms. "I did it!"

I kneeled and caught her in a hug, kissing her forehead.

She giggled.

"You be careful," I warned.

"Come play with me, Mommy."

"I can't, honey, not today. Mommy has to find a job."

"Okay." Serenity rushed back to the playground equipment and scaled the platforms again. Her quick forgiveness made me paste on a smile.

Yesterday's newspaper rustled. I opened the paper to the help wanted page and sighed. Our small town limited my choices. An advertisement at the bottom of the page caught my attention:

> *Part-Time Housekeeper*
> *Hunt's Christmas Tree Farm*
> *Contact Noel Medford at*
> *218-120-1224*

I reread the simple ad. The job would be enough for paying our debts yet allowed supper to be ready before Jake got home. Would this Noel let me bring Serenity?

"Mommy, can we go home?"

"We have to stop at the library again." I folded the paper around the ad and tucked it in my pocket.

Serenity didn't complain about the block-long walk but chattered about Christmas.

My heart shriveled. Would there be enough money for her presents this year? Last year I had secreted enough to buy her clothes and a toy from the thrift store. The joy on her face had been worth the risk. Now, Jake accounted for all his cash leaving no hope in pocketing again.

She let out a squeal and pointed at the library. Two men stood on ladders, stringing Christmas lights above the library's front entrance. Both gave a single nod and a 'happy holidays' greeting.

"Mewwy Chwistmas." Serenity waved.

We walked underneath and entered the entryway, finding stacked boxes pushed against the wall. Someone carried another one from the basement and sneezed.

"Bless you," I said automatically.

"Thank you," the librarian's voice replied, an eye peering beside the box. "I forgot how dusty it gets in the basement."

The librarian lowered the box onto the pile then wiped the dust off her hands using her pants. "Did you find a job?"

"May I use the phone?"

The elderly librarian smiled. "Of course, dear."

"Come, Serenity."

"But… I wanna help her-r-r," Serenity whined. "She—"

"I can keep her busy while you make your call." The librarian offered a hand, which Serenity accepted.

"Are you—"

"We'll be fine. Go make your call."

The librarian kneeled beside Serenity and whispered in her ear.

Serenity glanced at her. My daughter's nose crinkled as she giggled about what the older woman said. She waited while the librarian took a box off the stack and placed it on the floor. Together, they opened the box.

I climbed the steps and paused with a hand resting on the door handle. A pile of decorations lay beside them while Serenity and the librarian exchanged words about what they found inside the box. Serenity was fine. I pulled on the door handle and entered the library.

The telephone sat at the edge of a tidied desk. I laid out the ad and lifted the receiver, punching the numbers. My insides jiggled. Several long rings went unanswered, and I prepared to leave a message.

A male voice answered on the last ring. "This is Noel. How may I help you?"

"My name is Mary Edwards, and I'm calling about the housekeeper ad."

"When can you start?"

"You-you-you don't want to interview me?"

"Will tomorrow morning at nine work?"

"Yes." I removed a pen lying beside the keyboard and tore a sticky note off the pad. Though it had been years since I'd been there, I needed a refresher. "What's the address?"

"One-two-two-five-zero Mistletoe Lane. It's seven miles north on Highway twenty-five."

"I—is it okay I bring along my three-year-old daughter?" I swallowed at the idea of returning to the tree farm and working for the Hunts. Nick wouldn't be there … it had been ten years.

"She'd be delightful to have around the house. I look forward to meeting you and your daughter tomorrow morning, and we can talk more about what the job entails then. See you tomorrow."

"Bye."

The phone clicked against the cradle. I leaned back in the chair and stretched. Noel gave the job without an interview. Who did that? What if Noel decided he didn't like me after we talked tomorrow, especially when he learned I lied?

"Mommy, look." Serenity dragged behind a string of silver garland.

The librarian followed behind with a clear tote containing balls and snowflakes.

"Oh my, what do you have there?"

My daughter's foot tangled with the garland, and she stumbled. When Serenity righted herself, she pushed part of the garland toward me. "It's a gawland."

"Garland."

"Miss Gwace said we hang it on the desk."

"We've never introduced ourselves." The librarian set the box on the floor and outstretched a hand. "I'm Grace Harland."

"Mary Edwards. My daughter's name is Serenity." I shook Grace's hand. It was soft and warm and smooth, just like Grandma Hazel's had been.

Serenity tugged at the hem of my jacket. "Can we decowate at home?"

My stomach clenched into a knot. I had packed the sad reminders in a box at the back of a closet, which waited to be pieced together. "We'll have to make some, won't we?"

A smile crept across Serenity's face. She dug a ball out of the box and studied it, rotating it slowly. "Pwetty."

"Be careful."

Grace lifted the garland heap from the floor. "You can tape while she's looking at the balls."

Serenity hummed as she examined another ball.

I tore a strip of tape and attached the garland to the desk's end. Grace and I worked together, her holding the garland while I secured it.

A ball rolled. Serenity squealed and leapt away as the ball splintered into shards on the floor. Her small cry escalated into sobs. She flinched when Grace kneeled.

"Shh. It's okay," Grace murmured. "Accidents happen."

"I'm sorry. I'm so sorry," I said.

Grace laid a hand across my arm, stopping me from collecting the rest of the smashed ball. "You don't have to apologize. She didn't mean it."

I clamped my tongue between my teeth. The slight pressure on the covered bruise hurt, fresh from this morning's encounter.

Grace patted my arm, and I bit harder, but not enough to draw blood. "The balls were old, anyway."

"Is there anything I can do to help pay for the broken ball?"

Grace grabbed a tissue off her desk and dried Serenity's tears. "I'd like help decorating."

After Grace dried my daughter's tears, she lifted a red ball and held it in her palm. She smiled. "Here's another one for you."

Serenity touched the red ball but withdrew her fingers. "I hang it?"

The librarian nodded.

My daughter removed the ornament gingerly and cradled it. She ambled to the hung garland. When the ball dangled, Serenity took a step backward and chortled. "I decowated."

Her glee almost made me forget about the broken Christmas decorations at home.

Two

My husband moaned at the kitchen table. Elbows rested on the table while Jake brought his hands to his head and groaned, "O-o-oh… my head."

I dished the scrambled eggs and pancakes onto a plate, careful not to clink my spatula on the glass. As I set the plate in front of him, he seized my wrist.

"Put vodka in my orange juice."

I tried to tug my arm away, but he wouldn't let go.

Jake sneered and shoved my arm backward. "Get me aspirin too."

The tip of my tongue ran along my lips, moistening them. I dared not offer a response and bobbed my head in acknowledgment as I backed from the table. When I reached a safe distance, I turned around and retrieved the vodka bottle above the fridge. Only a quarter of the clear liquid remained. I poured vodka in the glass, the orange juice masking its appearance except by taste. I hoped it was enough. Jake's concoction usually contained more vodka than orange juice.

Before I could set the glass on the table, Jake snatched it and guzzled half of the mixed beverage. I strode to the cupboard that contained our over-the-counter medications. Inside, the aspirin pill bottle sat empty. I searched the cupboard but didn't find a replacement.

Jake moaned again.

I glanced behind. He wasn't watching. The allergy medication packaging slipped under my shaking fingers as I dislodged two from its blister.

"Today!"

I hurried and placed the allergy pills on the table. My stomach churned. Would he notice the shape difference of the pills?

Jake tossed the white pills in his mouth and took a long swig from the glass.

The wedding band twirled around my finger as I fidgeted. "We're out of aspirin."

"Charge it to the account."

"I-I-I can't… the account is past due."

Jake slapped his plate and glass off the table.

I jerked. The din produced a ringing clatter when the plate and glass wobbled back and forth before coming to a stop. Long ago I had learned Corelle dishes and plastic glasses stood up against Jake's temper.

"I'm trying here," Jake shouted. "If you'd quit spending our money."

The chair screeched across the linoleum flooring, landing with a bang. Jake grabbed my throat and pushed me against the fridge. His fingers inched a little deeper. "I bust my ass off because you're too lazy to work."

"Plea—" I clutched at his crushing grip. Dared I tell him I got a job? No, he'd drink that money away too.

Jake released his hold.

I leaned forward, coughing.

"I'm sorry." Jake raised a hand to my cheek. "You don't understand the stress I'm under."

I flinched as he caressed along my cheek, then my jaw.

Jake continued down my throat. He unfastened the three buttons on my shirt and slipped his hand inside, fondling my breast. "You're so beautiful it makes me crazy," he whispered.

Please, God. Let Serenity stay in her room.

My heart thumped wildly inside my chest at what he would do next. If hearts exploded out of chests, mine was on its way as its beats pulsated against my eardrums. The clock hands ticked together on eight. Was he going to work today?

"We should make another baby."

My muscles tightened. We couldn't afford another child, not with how much he spent on liquor.

"Jake." I forced a giggle. "You're going to be late."

"They can wait." His lips brushed against mine. Jake unbuttoned my pants and lifted me onto the counter.

"Stop. The neighbors will see."

"See what? That I love my wife?" Jake unzipped his pants.

"Daddy?" Serenity asked, her green eyes wide.

"Go back to your room," he snapped.

A sob choked out. "Hungwy."

"I'll get you something to eat, sweetie." I shimmied into my pants and sidestepped him.

A blow struck. "We're not finished."

"Please, she doesn't know any better."

Jake grabbed my hair and yanked until pain radiated into my neck and upper back.

Serenity cried louder.

"You're the reason she doesn't listen," he hissed, releasing my hair and giving a kick.

My knees thudded against the floor, the stinging sensation bringing instant tears. I should have known better. I should have encouraged Serenity back to her room. Pain always came when he didn't get his way with me.

"We'll finish this tonight." Jake swung once more and felled me like the trees at the Christmas tree farm.

The front door slammed. Our wedding picture fell off the wall and shattered. Through the tears I gazed upon the broken remnants lying on the floor that related to my life, unfixable. I deserved this. My jaw clenched.

"Mommy?"

Serenity needed me. Her presence provided the strength I needed to get up from the floor and continue living.

As I swept the slivers, it provided a reminder of how my dreams had been swept away after marrying Jake. I shouldn't have settled for him. Five years of waiting for a broken heart to heal hadn't been enough when I sought happiness with Jake.

Serenity hummed between bites of graham crackers.

Her innocence made my heart swell. If I hadn't married Jake, I wouldn't have had my daughter. Thank God for the small blessing in my life, or I wouldn't make it.

Please make it. Please make it there. My SUV rattled and clunked, worsening over the bumps on the highway. The gas gauge dipped below a quarter-tank and would be barely enough to make the trip home. Jake would find out about my job, if she died before we made it back to town.

"Chwistmas twees," Serenity shrieked, pointing at the evergreen forest.

I slowed, turning left at the Hunt's Christmas tree sign. Chainsaws revved in the distance as the car rolled along the long, narrow driveway. The majestic view nestled inside the woods hadn't changed in the ten years since I saw it last.

"Look, Mommy. Horsies!"

Clydesdale horses frolicked inside a corral attached to a worn barn. Clouds puffed around their noses. Noel hadn't mentioned where to park, so I parked beside the fence like I had done in the past.

Serenity unbuckled herself from her seat. By the time the back door opened, we had become spectators to six horses. They sniffed the air and neighed.

"Can I pet them?"

"Watch me." I held out a palm over the fence.

A whiskered nose cautiously lowered near my hand and gave a nudge when she decided there was no danger. My eyes watered at a long-ago memory I had buried. I stroked her. "Sorry girl, I don't have a treat for you."

Serenity stayed quiet.

I turned and found who she had been staring at, a man with a trimmed white beard. He could pass for Santa with his hat and red coat.

A smile crept across his face. "You've been around horses before."

"My grandparents raised them."

"You must be Mary. I'm Noel Medford." The Santa lookalike stepped forward and offered a hand. After we had shaken hands, Noel met my daughter at her eye-level. "And who might you be?"

"Are you Santa?"

A rich laugh permeated the air, joined by Serenity's high-pitched giggles. When their laughter diminished, Noel touched her nose and removed his finger after saying 'boop.'

Serenity's nose scrunched up and she giggled.

"Have you been a good girl this year, Serenity?"

Her eyes grew large. "How do you know my name?" she whispered.

"Santa knows everything." Noel withdrew a candy cane and waited until I nodded.

Serenity spun around. She raised the peppermint stick and gave a big smile. "I got candy."

"How about we go into the house?" Noel took her hand. "I have toys you can play with while your mommy and I visit."

A lump grew in my throat.

They conversed with each other as I trailed behind. Grandpa Bill and I used to walk this way during my childhood.

I paused on the porch steps. The two-story house with its wrap-around porch seemed enormous compared to my house. Returning to the tree farm was like coming home again, with the house sharing a resemblance to my grandparents' home down the highway. I stroked the bare pillars. "No decorations?"

"Tomorrow we get the shipment. Would you like to help?"

Serenity shook Noel's hand. "I help too."

"I have a special job for you, the Christmas tree."

Serenity dropped his hand, gawking at the evergreens in the distance. "All of them?"

Both Noel and I laughed.

"No, honey. I think he means the tree inside the house," I responded.

"Oh."

Noel gestured at the open door. "Shall we, ladies?"

Three

While the tree farm had been undecorated yesterday, today crates sat askew on the porch. Men tramped up and down the steps hauling large boxes while others attached fresh pine garland along the fences. Noel stood on the porch and gave instructions. When we approached, he was talking to a man and raised a finger at us to stop. When Noel finished the conversation, we exchanged a greeting.

An apple cider aroma permeated the air inside the house. Like the crates outside, totes lay strewn about in a messy yet orderly fashion. Across the tops of the totes, labels marked what room they belonged in.

A seven-foot-tall tree waited in front of the window for ornaments. Serenity tossed her coat onto the floor and raced across the living room to the tree. She stopped at the tree's bottom branch, her eyes traveling upwards. "Big tree."

"Serenity, please pick up your coat," I demanded.

Serenity remained still in her position.

"Please. Mister Noel doesn't like it when people throw their coats on the floor."

"You pick it up."

I stared. Had she really said that?

Noel placed a hand on Serenity's shoulder, and she swatted at it.

"Don't touch me."

My eyes closed. Serenity had heard Jake and me last night. Please don't say anything about Mommy and Daddy fighting.

"Do you like apple cider?" Noel asked.

"You got more candy?"

"If it's okay with your mommy, perhaps after we finish decorating. How about we pick up your jacket and hang it in the closet, then go get apple cider?"

"Okay." Serenity whirled around and scooped her coat off the floor, giving it to Noel. Her feet slapped across the hardwood and into the kitchen.

"You okay?" Noel asked.

"She's never done that before."

"Is everything all right at home?"

My mouth went dry. "Yeah, money's tight. But we're fine."

Noel tipped his head to the side and gazed but said nothing. He walked to the closet with Serenity's coat draped over his arm. After securing her jacket on a hanger, Noel padded toward the kitchen and hesitated in the doorway. "If you need to talk, I'm here to listen."

He disappeared into the kitchen.

Had he known about Jake? Maybe I should quit. I sighed. No, we needed the money.

I joined Noel and Serenity in the kitchen and found steaming mugs sitting on the table in front of them. The tidy kitchen had nothing broken or left behind to fix or clean, unlike mine. No cabinet doors sagged or were cracked, and clean dishes were stacked neatly beside the sink.

The window above the sink came with a view of a skating pond and the woods. It was scenery that seemed to come out of a professional photograph, and one I had memorized long ago. A faint laughter echoed. I shouldn't have come back here.

"Cups are in the cupboard to the right of the sink, if you'd like some apple cider," Noel said.

I reached for a mug when Serenity yelped, followed by a crash.

"Ow…" she whimpered, her hands clasped over her lips.

"Did you burn your mouth?" I asked.

Serenity nodded with tears welling.

I ran cold water in a glass and gave it to her. "Here, the cold water should help."

"Accidents happen." Noel squatted, towel in hand.

Serenity flinched.

"I can clean it up."

"No, it's my fault. I should have let it cool before giving it to her." Noel glanced at a clock on the wall beside the doorway and then mopped the spill with the towel. "I should get back to work."

"What would you like me to do?"

"You ladies can decorate the main floor. After I'm finished outside, I'll decorate the second floor."

"If you'd like, I can do that tomorrow."

Noel shook his head. "It's best if I do it. We have a guest staying with us that's recovering, and I need to talk to him about you."

A guest? It had been years since a Hunt lived here. I gazed past the kitchen's doorway and into the living room. Who'd want to recover at a tree farm? If they did, it would be nice if they brought life back into this empty home.

More memories revealed themselves as I dusted off an eight-track player. I plugged the relic in and removed a Christmas tape from inside the tote. "Frosty the Snowman" began playing.

Serenity rustled nearby and clapped her hands. "Sing, Mommy."

I squeezed my eyes shut and whispered past the bulging lump in my throat. "Not right now, honey."

Her little hands warmed my cheeks. When she spoke, peppermint breath gently puffed against my face. "Why you sad?"

"Mommy misses Grandma."

"Grand… ma?"

I hugged her, sniffling. Her never meeting my family tore at my heart, especially since she'd never heard of the word grandma. When Serenity was born, Jake's mom had demanded being called Nana.

Mom and Dad would have loved being grandparents. It wasn't fair they had died when I was a teenager, and that my grandparents had died before I was pregnant with Serenity.

"Don't cwy." Serenity rubbed my tear trails.

"My grandma and I used to play Christmas music while we decorated. Should we do that?"

Serenity swayed. "And dance?"

I smiled. My daughter resembled Grandma Hazel so much that I often wondered if Serenity was her reincarnated. I snatched her hands, and we twirled until we fell to the floor giggling. A clatter came from the staircase.

"Noel? Is that you?" a familiar voice asked.

I responded, "Noel's outside at the moment."

Someone rushed back upstairs. The man almost resembled…

No, it couldn't be…

Serenity stared with widened eyes. "Who was that, Mommy?"

"I think it's Mister Noel's guest."

"He didn't say hi." Serenity crossed her arms, transforming her appearance into the famous pouting stance. "I find him."

"Serenity… stay here."

"Humph." She plopped down on the couch between the clutter and didn't move when I held a Christmas ball.

I hummed along with the eight-track player while circling the tree and hanging ornaments. Each ornament represented a moment in time for the Hunts. It saddened me to see a prominent family gone from Spruce Point, except for the lone Balthazar Hunt.

Serenity watched through narrowed eyes.

I turned my back toward her and fussed over the decorations' placement. After I finished, I asked, "How does it look?"

No answer. She was giving me the silent treatment again.

I sighed and finished manipulating a light strand. The eight-track tape reached the end and stopped, waiting for a new tape. Silence loomed in the room.

"Serenity?"

When she didn't respond, my gaze shifted to the couch. Her spot was empty. "Honey? Where are you?"

I searched the living room and kitchen where she might have hidden but didn't find her. Perhaps she was in the bathroom. I swallowed.

A scream came from upstairs, followed by barking. "Puppy!"

My heart, along with my feet, flew up the stairs and through the hallway to the first bedroom. Noel had never mentioned a dog in the house. I skidded to a stop on the hardwood floor.

Serenity giggled as a golden retriever licked her face, its tail wagging furiously. A leather harness encompassed the dog's body with a long handle that said, 'working dog, please don't pet me.'

"His name is Ford," a well-known male voice said to Serenity.

I blinked. "Nick?"

It couldn't be. Nick had left Spruce Point and joined the army. My already fast heartbeat roared until I thought it might tear through my chest. Age had enhanced his handsome figure.

"Who is this?"

Why was he wearing sunglasses? I tiptoed closer. "It's Mary. What are you doing here?"

Nick stiffened, clenching the dog's harness tighter until his fingers blanched. "Is this your daughter with Jake?"

"Her name is Serenity."

"Take her and leave."

"I-I-I'm sorry." I parted my daughter and his dog. "What happened to you?"

"I said, 'take her and leave.'"

"We're leaving." I nudged Serenity into the hallway. If I had known Nick was here, I would have never answered Noel's ad.

Serenity and I trudged down the stairs, her with folded arms across her chest. At the bottom step, she faced me. "Mommy? Why he mad?"

I slumped on the stairs and draped a hand on each of her shoulders. Her green eyes reflected an eagerness for an answer. Serenity must never know. I moistened my lips. "Don't tell Daddy we were here."

Four

I stood at the closet and inventoried what we had for Christmas decorations. The tree needed to be mended, and ornaments had to be glued and fixed before decorating it. Hands kneaded my shoulders, and I flinched at the massage's roughness. Tingles tickled the back of my neck, traveling upward where Jake kissed. I shrugged to get him to stop. "Jake."

Jake gave one last kiss. "What are you doing?"

"I'm digging out our Christmas stuff." I pointed at an artificial tree in the closet that had the top draping over the bottom.

"Oh, no… it's bwoken," Serenity said, staring with wide eyes. She rubbed a branch. "And dead."

Jake and I laughed. He crouched in front of her. "It's not real, sweetheart."

"What's weal?"

Please don't tell him about the tree farm. Please, please, please. I fidgeted with the dangling treetop.

"Real means alive, like the trees outside."

"I saw lots of Chwistmas trees outside, Daddy."

Jake ruffled her hair. "You did? Where'd you see them?"

"In the car."

"Oh, I see." Jake tipped his head toward me and glared. "Mary … why were you driving?"

My mouth went dry. "I took Serenity for a country drive."

"Did she ask?"

"I thought she might enjoy getting out of town."

Jake rose, grabbing and twisting my arm. "Don't lie. You were leaving me."

"I'd never leave you."

"Are you sure about that?" Jake rotated my arm farther until a radiating pain seared upward.

"I love you."

"Do you love me more than him?"

"Yes."

Jake released my arm and gave it a shove. "If he ever comes back, I guess we'll find out how much more you love me."

I blinked, tears threatening to overflow. *He never hurt me or drank like you do.*

"I think we should put the tree in Serenity's bedroom." My husband lifted the tree as if he hadn't twisted my arm.

Serenity shook her head with a grin. "No-o-o…"

"The kitchen?"

"Silly Daddy. The living woom."

"You show me."

Carrying the tree, Jake followed her.

I rolled my sleeve and inspected the forming handprint. This one would take longer than the others to heal. *Be glad he didn't break it, like you broke Mom* and Dad. Pangs pulled at my heart at how much I missed them.

"Mommy, mommy, mommy." Serenity dashed into the hallway and grabbed my hand. She led me to the living room, where Jake tweaked the tree top until it was fixed. "Come look."

"Got it fixed." My husband admired what had been broken by him last year and now fixed this year.

I wished the ornaments were as easy to fix.

Jake rubbed his hands together. "Who wants to decorate?"

Serenity bounced, a hand raised above her head. "Me, me, me."

I swallowed at what would happen next when he learned about the decorations' plight. "I-I-I can't find them."

Jake huffed, muttering something. He vanished from the room and returned with a taped box labelled 'ornaments.' "They're right here."

I should have stuffed them farther in the closet.

"Daddy found them." Jake opened the box. He lifted a soldier that was in two pieces, dropped it, and rummaged through the rest. "Are they all broken?"

"I haven't glued them together yet."

You broke them.

Jake threw the box, fragments spilling onto the carpet. "I spend time with my family, and you do this shit. I'm going to Orson's."

You could have bought new ornaments.

I said nothing and began collecting the shards, putting them in the box.

A boot pinned my hand. As Jake ground his boot, a sharp edge pierced the skin of my palm and lodged itself in the meat.

"Aren't you going to give me a goodbye kiss?"

"Please stop," I whispered toward the floor.

"What's that?"

"You're hurting me."

Jake grabbed my jaw and smashed his lips against mine. "Now, was that so bad?"

"Should we expect you for supper?" The corners of my mouth forced an upward curve. "I'm making your favorite."

"Chicken and dumplings? I'm not sure, but I'll try."

That was code for 'I'll be at the bar till closing.'

The fake smile slipped away as he retrieved his coat beside the door and left. I held my palm over the sink and rinsed the blood off, examining it for any embedded glass. None appeared in the wound. My wound bandaged, I finished collecting the broken pieces.

After an hour of gluing with little results, I cleaned the mess and readied Serenity for a visit to the library.

Serenity stomped her boots on the mat inside the entryway, each stomp causing an echo in the building.

"Shh…" I pressed a finger against my lips. "Wipe your boots like this."

I rubbed the soles back and forth in a gentle motion on the rug. Before I finished, Serenity had trudged up the steps and outstretched her arms as she tried to pull the library's heavy door with no success.

She rapped on the glass.

"Serenity, wait. I'm coming."

Noel's face appeared, and he smiled, pushing the door open. "Well, look who's here, Serenity."

My daughter giggled.

"Come on in. Miss Grace and I are having coffee and visiting."

"That man made Mommy cwy." Serenity placed her hands on her hips.

"Oh?"

"Go play," I whispered in her ear.

"But Mommy, I saw you."

"Serenity…"

Her arms crossed, and Serenity flicked her hair back with a harrumph then marched inside.

I snatched the hat she had dropped on the floor. "Sorry. Serenity snuck upstairs yesterday while I was decorating the tree. When she screamed, I found Nick's dog licking her."

"Stop. It's okay." Noel clasped my hand within his, stopping me from wringing Serenity's hat. "I should have told you sooner."

"What happened to him?"

"Let's sit at the table. Do you drink coffee?"

My stomach churned. Nick had changed since we were together in our young and carefree days.

"Mary? Are you all right?"

I nodded. "I was just remembering what he was like before…"

Grace sat at a small circular table while Serenity stacked blocks behind her. We would have to talk quietly.

The coffee pot clinked against the cup as Grace poured. "Do you want sugar or creamer?"

"Both, if you've got it."

Grace laid a spoon on a napkin and then set the creamer and sugar beside it. "What was it like seeing him again?"

"Who?" I added creamer and a spoonful of sugar and stared at the light and dark swirl mixing.

Noel sat across the table. "Nick Hunt."

"How—"

"My son-in-law, Christian, told me you and Nick had history," Noel said. "I should have told you over the phone."

I took a long sip from my cup. Christian married Noel's daughter? I never thought he'd marry again, not after Jenny drowned sixteen years ago.

"Nick needs you."

"I… I can't. I'm married."

Grace grasped my hand and gave a squeeze. "If anyone can help him, it's you and that darling daughter of yours."

"Why me?"

"Since losing his sight, Nick… well, he's never recovered." Noel sighed. "Christian's tasked me with helping him, but I'm afraid my efforts haven't gone far."

"What happened?"

"IED explosion. That's all we know because he won't talk about it."

Warmth seeped through the coffee mug. The heat didn't ward off the deep chill within that Nick had been in a hospital somewhere, and I wasn't there. Nick had been when I…

"Mary?" Grace asked.

I blinked. "Nick won't confide in me. After he learned Serenity was my daughter, he kicked us out of his room."

"Please, you're our only miracle," Noel pleaded.

"How?"

Noel gestured at Serenity. "Leave it to her."

Five

Shoes scraped and nails clicked against the hardwood floor. My daughter skipped as she followed Nick and Ford toward the kitchen. Nick murmured to Ford, and both stopped. Serenity stayed hidden behind them. Nick and his guide dog remained standing in the kitchen doorway for a minute when he cleared his throat. "Your daughter is stubborn."

Laughter streamed from my throat until tears formed. Stubborn described my daughter all right. I took a deep breath, stifling the laughter that wanted to continue. "She's like Grandma Hazel."

"I don't remember her being that stubborn."

"If Serenity's bothered you, I'm sorry. I'll make sure she stays downstairs."

"No, it's nice having the company." Nick fidgeted with Ford's leash. "I uh… wanted to… um…"

"Tell her you're sowwy," Serenity whispered in her shrill voice.

"I'm sorry."

His blue eyes flickered back and forth. The man I had dated in high school ceased to exist inside him now. Though his eyes were unseeing, they still reflected something broken within. Grandma Hazel always said you could see someone's brokenness by reading their eyes. Thank goodness Nick couldn't read mine.

A decade later and something inside my closed heart cracked with feelings once buried. Jake must never learn that Nick was back. I swallowed. He would taunt me about proving my love to him.

"Mary."

I gasped. "What'd you say?"

"Do you accept my apology?"

"Serenity, honey, go play. Mommy and Nick need to talk."

"Can Ford play too?"

Nick kneeled. His hand sought for something, then stopped when it found Serenity's shoulder. "Ford has to stay with me in case I need help. He's my eyes now."

"Okay." Serenity whirled around and scampered off to the toy box in the living room.

Ford whined.

Nick stroked the golden retriever's head. "I'm sorry, boy. But you know the rules."

A tingle started at the back of my neck and shuddered its way through my scalp. I squeezed my eyes shut. His fingers combed through my hair with each caress, as if it had happened yesterday.

"You okay?"

The intimate memory vanished. Heat suffused my face, growing hotter like I'd been standing in front of the fireplace for too long. "Why'd you come back?"

"Nowhere to go. Plus, I'm no use to the army blind. Why *are you* here?"

"I needed a job."

"What's the matter? Jake's job doesn't pay enough?" Nick jeered.

I stiffened. "You know nothing."

"Know anything? I joined the army to give us—" his voice cracked.

"After— you left me! You disappeared and made me deal with it alone."

"Who, Mommy?" Serenity peered through the kitchen doorway from the living room.

One day I would take Serenity to his gravesite and tell her about him. Until then, she must never be told. "Serenity, what did I tell you about listening to adult talk?"

The front door closed. "Who wants to help me feed the horses?" Noel asked.

"Me, me, me."

"Certainly not Serenity," Noel teased.

Serenity giggled as Noel scooped her up into his arms. He tickled her with his beard and set her back on the floor. "Go put on your coat while I talk to your mommy."

Her footsteps thumped against the floor. Noel watched her. "I hope it's all right if I take her to feed the Clydesdales."

"Yeah, Nick and I are finished talking."

"Nick, it's nice to see you down here."

"Like I had a choice," Nick grumbled. "Little girl wouldn't stop pestering me about an apology."

Noel laughed.

As hard as I tried, his laugh brought a genuine smile.

Serenity tugged at Noel's hand and led him away to the entryway. "I'm weady. Bye, Nick. Bye, Mommy."

"Does she look like Grandma Hazel?" Nick asked.

"Yeah, except for her eyes. Those are mine."

"Do you ever wonder what… what he'd—"

"Don't."

"I miss him."

"I miss him too." The whisper escaped from my lips. "Excuse me. I need to clean your room."

I sidestepped Nick and paused when the familiar shape of his hand brushed along mine. Our fingers interlaced with each other without thought. Jake. You're married to Jake.

"Mary."

"What?"

"I'm sorry for hurting you, leaving like I did without a goodbye." Nick caressed the top of my hand then freed it.

I never responded but continued through the living room and up the stairs. Once I reached Nick's bedroom, the tears fell.

It's my fault he died. I slumped onto the bed. He had needed me, and I wasn't there because of succumbing to exhaustion. If I hadn't, I could have saved him.

A golden blur nudged a head under my hand.

Ford. I wrapped my arms around his neck and nuzzled against the soft fur. He provided the solace I needed. When I finished, I used a shirt sleeve to dry my face. Ford never moved, his soft brown eyes studying me.

I scratched behind his ears. "Thanks, boy. Go find Nick."

Ford's harness jangled as he padded out of the room. Nick must have sent him, the gesture bringing a small smile. If Nick only knew how long I waited before concluding he was never coming back. Maybe he'd forgive me then.

"How'd it go today?" Noel lowered his newspaper as I entered the living room.

The afternoon at the tree farm had crept by yet sped into twilight with all that needed cleaning. I gaped, unsure what he meant—with cleaning, Nick, or my daughter?

Noel folded the paper and set it on the end table. His hazel eyes traveled to Serenity playing near the fireplace. A smile curled upon his face. "According to Christian, it's been a long time since this house had a child in it."

Serenity provided sound effects as she played with her dolls near the Christmas tree. Her playing there made for a beautiful holiday scene between the tree and the decorations above the lit fireplace. The backdrop made it a picture where people would take family Christmas photos. When was the last Christmas picture our family had taken? Serenity's first Christmas?

"You were right about her."

"Nick still cares about you." Noel's gaze drifted to the partially exposed bruise around my wrist. "Seems to me you both need a friend."

I pulled my sleeve over the bruise. "That's from falling on the ice."

The lie flitted easily off my tongue. It bothered me how long I had been creating excuses for injuries. Nobody understood I deserved it. I prepared for the accusation Noel would make about spousal abuse.

Noel never did. Instead, he rummaged for something inside his coat, which lay draped on the armrest. He withdrew a thick manila envelope from the pocket. "Here's cash for your services."

"You're firing me?"

"No, I'm sure you need cash more than a check."

I took the envelope and unfastened the flap, gasping at the stack of twenties hidden within. "All this for two days' work? This is too much." I tried foisting it back on him.

"You need it." Noel ignored the envelope I shoved back at him. "Keep it. You might need it for Christmas presents."

"Thanks. I'm not sure how else I can thank you…"

"Just keep bringing her."

I nodded. "Serenity, honey, it's time to go home and make supper for Daddy."

The envelope tucked safely in the lining of my coat. I removed Serenity's jacket from the closet while she put away the dolls in a toy box someone had placed in the living room since we decorated. I suspected Noel. When she finished cleaning, I held out her coat.

Serenity zipped her jacket. "I say goodbye to Nick."

"He doesn't want to be bothered."

Serenity sprinted toward the steps and vanished upstairs, calling for Ford.

The guide dog barked.

I imagined the golden retriever licking her face. For her, I think it was more about saying goodbye to Ford than Nick. Too bad we couldn't afford a dog.

"You should visit Grace tomorrow," Noel said.

"You don't want me to come in tomorrow?"

"I have a feeling you two could use each other's company."

Serenity reappeared at the top of the stairs and paused for a brief second. She bounded down, one step at a time.

I rolled my lips inward between my teeth. Don't fall. We couldn't go back to the emergency room this soon.

"Please don't jump." Nick placed a hand on the banister and glided it along, stopping whenever Serenity landed.

Serenity stopped midway on the staircase. "Why?"

"I'm sure it scares your mom."

"She's always scared."

My breath stuck in my throat. Please, please, please don't mention Jake hitting us. We would have to talk later about keeping secrets.

"Oh yeah? What is she scared—"

I interrupted, "Serenity, honey, we need to get going."

"I stay here," she whined.

"Don't you want to see Daddy?"

"No."

Nick stepped down and placed a free hand on her back. "I promise that Ford and I won't go anywhere, and we'll be here when you come back to visit. Right now, I'm betting your daddy would like to see you when he gets home from work."

"He never home."

"Serenity," I pleaded, tipping my head and giving my best 'be quiet' look.

"Oh? Where does he go?" Nick asked.

I started for the stairs. "It's time to go home."

"Owson's."

Too late.

Nick slumped onto the step. "What'd you say? Is that true, Mary?"

I reached for Serenity and gave a slight tug to nudge her into moving. "We're leaving."

"Mary?"

I continued prodding Serenity toward the front door without answering Nick. "We'll see you Friday."

Six

Fingers tugged at my underwear and slid them downward. "Jake, it's late," I mumbled, still half-asleep.

His weight straddled atop my hips. In the faint street light glow, Jake divested his shirt and tossed it on the bedroom floor. He never responded to my remark.

I raised my head and shoulders off the bed by using my elbows, "Get off me."

Jake fumbled below.

"Stop it." I squirmed.

It was no use. He was stronger than me.

Jake leaned forward as he gripped my wrists and pinned them above my head. His rank breath wafted into my nose. "Nick Hunt's back in town. Did you know?"

"No." I swallowed. Jake would kill me if he found out I worked at the tree farm.

Jake squeezed my wrists tighter until the joints popped. "Don't lie to me. You did, didn't you?"

"I-I-I thought it a rumor."

"Just remember, you're mine."

I braced myself, rolling my lips between my teeth and clamping down on them. Don't fight. It would be over soon enough.

Jake jammed himself inside, yet I lurched.

As he pecked back and forth, I stared at the cracks in the ceiling. That one looked like it had gotten bigger. It and another crack formed a shape like a horse. I closed my eyes and imagined my horse at Grandma and Grandpa's farm.

Cotton galloped across the pasture and jumped the fence in one majestic leap. I understood why now. She wanted to be free. She had been so trusting when I tricked her back into the corral.

The bed banged against the wall. Please don't let Serenity hear.

Jake panted, moving faster and faster until my body shook like a jackhammer.

Please, God, let him finish soon. A throb began. I clenched my jaw and endured the stinging pain. In his state, it wouldn't be much longer.

A throaty roar grew louder, dying as Jake gave one last jab. He sniggered and collapsed, panting. "When he sees you pregnant, he'll remember you're mine."

My fingers wavered. He doesn't know Nick's blind. Should I tell him?

Jake flipped over onto his side of the bed and yanked the covers past his waist.

I lay there paralyzed if I moved that he'd wake and punish me again. Tears cascaded down my cheeks. Life would have been different if Nick hadn't left. Why'd he leave me? Maybe, this was God's punishment, taking away everyone I've loved.

An assortment of brochures lined the magazine rack in the library's entryway. I pressed shaky fingers against my legs. The words 'domestic abuse' and 'alcohol' screamed off the covers. I held my breath and let those words wash over me. Perhaps I should try Al-Anon. What was the point? Jake would never stop drinking.

Did the other Al-Anon members' spouses abuse them too in a drunken rage?

The thin pamphlet crinkled between my fingertips. I sighed. The meetings were held in the evenings. With Jake's unpredictability of being home, I'd never be able to attend without getting caught.

I jerked at the slight tug on my hand.

"Mommy?" Serenity asked. "You scared?"

My lips curled inward as I considered how to answer. I closed my eyes. Would Jake make it for supper tonight, or would he stumble home in the early morning hours with a repeat performance?

I winced at the reminder when I shifted the weight from one foot to the other.

"Mary, what's wrong?" asked Grace, who stood with a box of cupcakes.

I composed myself and feigned a small smile. "Nothing. Just got emotional reading the pamphlets is all."

"Come celebrate with me." Grace juggled the box of cupcakes while she unlocked the door.

"Miss Gwace, is it your birthday?"

"Sometimes a person needs cake to celebrate the good things in life. Say, I heard little girls like cupcakes? Is that true?"

Serenity giggled. "With pink fwosting."

"I'll get the door," I said.

Serenity skipped behind Grace. With each flip of the light switch, the library awakened for its human companions.

My daughter hung her coat without being told. Her boots clomped against the floor and stopped when she seated herself at the kids' table.

After Grace gave her a glass of water and cupcake, she joined me at the adult table. We sipped coffee with our cupcakes.

"Forty-five years ago on this day, my sisters rescued me and my son from my abusive husband." Grace took a bite and pushed her plate aside. She chewed for a second. "I celebrate to remind myself that my life changed for the better that day."

"How'd you do it?"

"My sisters and their husbands came while Carter was at work and packed me up. At first, I protested, saying it wasn't that bad, but they refused to listen."

"Does your son remember?"

"I was pregnant with him at the time and never told him about his biological father until he was an adult." Grace paused, taking a sip of coffee. "Even then, I didn't want to tell him."

I nodded, unsure of what to say. Had Noel told her about the bruise on my arm?

Grace took another bite of her cupcake. We sat in silence as she savored it, and when Grace swallowed, she spoke again. "Now, I treat life like I treat an excellent piece of cake. Both are to be relished."

Not me, I deserved punishment. "I'm glad you overcame a bad situation."

"In honor of my sisters, now, I devote my life to helping abused women in my free time."

"How many?"

"Oh, I've lost count. That's why Noel was here the other day making a donation for my cause." Grace took a napkin and dabbed her glistening eyes. "I couldn't save all of them."

A slight pressure wedged itself in my throat. Serenity and I needed help. I pinched the fabric of my jeans to contain our secret. "I'm sure they still appreciated you trying."

"Thanks. I often wonder if I could have done more to save them." Grace sniffled.

"Women like that have to want to leave an abusive relationship." I fidgeted with the cupcake liner. Not me, I had to stay. I had to be punished for the deaths I caused.

Grace extended a hand across the table. When I offered mine, she covered it with both hands and whispered, "I'm ruining a perfectly good celebration with sadness. Thank you for being here with me."

Jake's name bubbled further up my throat. The reminders of my parents' mangled bodies kept it from spilling out. I shouldn't have called them during the blizzard. It was my fault they died. Just like it was my fault that *he*…

Ten years since he died, and I still couldn't say his name. Then Nick left and enlisted in the army, abandoning me during our family's time of grief. I deserved the pain. He blamed me.

I managed a smile. "Serenity and I enjoy visiting you."

Pretending was easier than an explanation for my sadness. Grace was the closest I'd been in divulging my shame. I admired her courage, the mettle she had in leaving an abusive husband while pregnant, and her resolve for helping other women in the same situation. She never killed people like me, either.

Seven

The engine whined a groan but refused to start. I slammed my palms on the steering wheel and leaned my forehead on top. Noel was in town running errands and wouldn't be back for another two to three hours. I couldn't possibly disturb another employee to give us a ride home. What would I tell Jake?

"Come on." I cranked the key in the ignition again.

"It's Nick and Ford," Serenity exclaimed.

I glanced through the windshield and held my breath as Ford led Nick. It was the first time I had seen the duo at work, and mixed emotions clouded my vision.

Nick knocked on the window.

I sniffled and wiped my eyes, a habit I had developed over the years since Nick had left.

He rapped on the window again.

I pulled the handle and pushed the car door open a crack. "Hey."

Ford wriggled his snout through the gap. His snout lay on my lap, and he gave those 'pet me' eyes. When I didn't, he poked his nose against my hand.

"Car trouble?" Nick asked.

"It doesn't want to start."

"Pop the hood."

Ford cocked his head as I jerked the worn tab, and the hood flipped upward with a shudder.

"Come on," Nick said to Ford.

Nick skimmed his fingertips along the car's body and stopped at the grill. He fidgeted underneath the slightly opened hood until the latch released. The hood rose, blocking my view. "Try starting it."

I turned the ignition switch. The engine made the same noise, and I sighed. Please let Nick be able to fix it. It had been over a decade since he worked on my SUV.

"It's your belt."

"Are you sure?"

I joined them in front of the opened hood and examined the engine. Nick had tried to teach me the inner workings in the past, but it remained a foreign language.

"Hold this for a minute." He held out the leather loop to Ford's leash.

Our fingers brushed against each other, and I took the leash, ignoring the racing tingle along my nape. Time had done nothing for our attraction. We were broken soulmates.

Nick pushed his sleeves up and touched various parts on the engine while muttering, "water pump… carburetor… there you are."

"What is it?"

"You have a loose spark plug wire. I can't believe you're still driving your SUV that your grandparents bought for you in high school." Nick chuckled. "I'd recognize that engine anywhere."

"If it weren't for them, I wouldn't have wheels."

"Jake won't buy you a new car?" Nick dry washed his hands and finished by wiping them on his jeans.

Goosebumps prickled across my arms. If he only knew what Jake does to us. I faked a smile. "Money's tight right now."

"You don't have to lie. Is it true?"

I sucked in a breath.

"Is Jake drinking again?"

Nick reached out and groped the air until he found my arm. "How bad?"

"Jake's fine." I slipped Ford's leash into his hand and pulled away, opening the car door. "We have to go."

Nick shut the hood. "Want me to talk to him?"

"Please don't."

"See you tomorrow then."

The car started with no protesting. I shifted the gear into reverse, and while I backed up, Nick waved. He continued when I turned the car around. In the rear-view mirror he quit waving and headed toward the porch steps.

I eased the car to a slow roll.

Nick tripped on the steps, and down he went. Ford stood beside him.

I hit the brakes and jerked the shifter into park. "Stay right here, honey. Mommy needs to help Nick."

"I—"

The car door cut off Serenity's whine. I loped the short distance and reached Nick by the time he rose. "Are you okay?"

"Don't!" Nick motioned with his arm, fending me off.

I laid a hand on his shoulder. Another tingle tickled the back of my neck, and I snatched my hand back. Each touch we shared since Nick's return sparked the reminder of what we had all those years ago. I loved Jake, but it was a different kind. The cruel past couldn't be changed.

Nick licked his lips. "I'm still learning how to get around without my eyes."

"Is… is it hard?"

"Is there a choice?" he shrugged.

The tears welled. His famous Hunts' blue eyes would never enjoy the world's beauty again. "I guess not," I whispered.

"I don't need your pity. If we would have married, I still wouldn't want your pity."

"I wish I could have been there when it happened."

"Why?" Nick snorted. "You married Jake."

"Five years! I waited for five long years, and you never came back. So, yeah, I moved on— not by choice."

"I— You— Serenity's waiting." His voice grew frosty.

Without speaking another word, I stomped back to my car and mocked Nick under my breath. He was an idiot. I had held onto memories of our beautiful life together, and in the end, memories couldn't console me when my grandparents died. Jake had.

The car tires skidded on the gravel driveway. I clenched my jaw. Did Nick think I had forgotten about him after he left?

Serenity hummed "Frosty the Snowman" as she glanced out the window. She stopped. "Mommy?"

"Yeah, sweetie?"

"Can we sing and dance?"

A half-choked sob and laugh burst forth. I pulled into an approach off the highway and parked.

Serenity's little green eyes twinkled. They responded like Grandma Hazel's did when she looked back and anxiously waited to see what I would say.

"How about I show you where Grandma and Grandpa used to live?"

"Oh yes," she squealed.

"It'll be our secret, okay?"

"What's secret?"

"It means you can't tell anyone we were there," I explained. What kind of mother was I, teaching a three-year-old to lie?

The gas needle hovered just above empty. I would barely have enough to make it back to town but kept driving. Another mile of gravel and crossing a small bridge, we arrived at the place that was once my grandparents' farm.

A large, rectangular dumpster sat in the yard. Pickups and trailers marked 'construction' lined the driveway. Pounding and sawing came from inside the house. The faded sold sign in the window was gone.

Serenity gasped. "He's throwing away the potty."

Two men heaved the old porcelain toilet into the dumpster. When they turned around, the one worker headed toward us.

I opened the car door and greeted him.

"What can I help you with?" he asked.

"I used to live here. Is the new owner remodeling?"

"Somewhat. Most of it is being restored though." The man stared at the two-story house. "I'm afraid I can't let you traipse down memory lane. It's too dangerous between men working and the mess. Sorry."

"Who's the owner?"

"I can't give you that information, but we usually deal with his assistant. All I know is the guy requested keeping the originals to the house."

"Oh." I stared at the dilapidated barn that had once housed my grandparents' horses. A lump formed in my throat. If Jake and I had taken over the business, we would have lost it to foreclosure too. Grandma and Grandpa never liked him. I should have listened to them about staying away from him.

Serenity's pink coat flashed at the edge of my peripheral.

"Hey, you can't go in there," the man shouted.

"Serenity, get back here now."

My daughter charged forward and slipped through the slightly opened barn door.

The man sprinted. "That barn's dangerous."

I trotted behind and kept calling her name.

The man wrested the sliding door, grunting as he widened his stance. He couldn't budge the door.

Serenity shrieked, "Mommy."

I wedged through the crack and wriggled inside. Debris crunched underneath my snow boots. Dim light filtered through the broken, dirty windows, outlining the shadows of my past. What was all this stuff doing in here?

"Look, Mommy." Serenity stood at a crib, her fingers wrapped around the dusty spindles. "I finds a baby cwib."

A sob burst through, and my hands clasped over my mouth. Nick had made that crib when...

Grandpa lied. He didn't get rid of the crib like I had asked.

I braced myself against a post. Had Grandpa kept it hidden in the barn all these years?

"Daddy say you have baby soon."

I shook my head. "Not yet, sweetie. Would you like a brother or sister?"

Serenity wrinkled her nose and slid her hands up and down along the bars. "Who baby this?"

"I don't know." The lie flicked off my tongue like the others. I traced the ridges along the dusty railing and closed my eyes. What seemed like yesterday's dreams played its recording like a punishment for looking at the future.

The airplane mobile tinkled. He'd squeal and kick his arms and legs as it spun above.

Arms wrapped around my legs. "Why you sad?"

I glanced at Serenity's sweet face. "It makes me sad to see something pretty like this in a barn."

Nick and I had been naïve in planning our future for a family together. Then death shattered our dreams.

"Take it."

"It doesn't belong to us, honey. If we take it without asking, then it's stealing and we can go to jail for that."

"Oh," she said. "Let's ask."

"No, I don't know who owns it. We need to get home and make supper for Daddy." I pressed against her back and prodded Serenity toward the door.

"Maybe Daddy does."

"Remember, we can't tell him we were here." Please, God. Don't let her mention the crib to Jake.

Eight

Serenity sang along with "Tale as Old as Time" as she watched *Beauty and the Beast*, her volume increasing. She was going to wake Jake.

I dashed toward the TV, trying to shush her.

"Be quiet," Jake snarled.

Too late. The beast had emerged from our bedroom, and he glared at Serenity, then at me.

Our daughter twirled, unaware she had woken him from another late-night stupor. She stopped and reached for him with a smile. "Dance with me, Daddy."

My heart pattered against my ribs. Jake stood in yesterday's rumpled clothes, his narrowed eyes drifting to her waiting hand. Please don't hit her. I grabbed Serenity's shoulders and nudged her away. "Daddy needs to get ready for work."

"I'm not going in today," Jake muttered.

I murmured in Serenity's ear. "You gotta be quiet today. Daddy's sick."

"But… but I wanna dance," Serenity whined.

"How 'bout we dance this afternoon when Daddy's better?"

Serenity folded her arms across her chest, and she stuck out her bottom lip. She plopped onto the floor and grabbed two dolls, babbling on about a conversation between them.

Jake scowled.

I swallowed. "Serenity, you've got to be quiet."

Jake shuffled to the kitchen and slumped into the chair, leaning his elbows against the table. When Serenity whined, his fist slammed against the table. "Shut her up!"

"She doesn't know any better, Jake."

Jake rose, teetering until he steadied himself by using the table's edge. He unbuckled his belt and removed it. "She will when I'm finished."

"Jake, no." I cut him off as he moved toward Serenity, standing between him and our daughter. "I promise she'll stay quiet for the rest of the day."

"She needs to be punished," he snapped. "Get out of my way."

"It's my fault, I should have told her you were sleeping."

Jake raised the belt above his head.

My arms barely protected my head when the force struck with a crack. I sucked in a breath. The stinging sensation pulsated, alternating between dull and sharp.

"Move," Jake shouted.

I spun around and covered Serenity with my body.

As Jake thrashed harder and faster, each whip cut deeper against my back until it burned. Serenity's screams pierced my ears. We had to get out of here. Our coats and boots sat ready at the door in case of emergencies. I lifted Serenity and poised to run when he raised the belt.

Jake continued striking and showed no signs of slowing. Occasionally the whip whizzed by, hitting the floor with a clang instead of my back. "Maybe next time you'll think twice before protecting that brat!"

I readjusted Serenity and jostled toward the door. Stumbling, I released our daughter and shoved her forward. "Open the door."

A kick knocked me down, the floor stinging my palms and knees. My mind rebelled. Give up.

"Mommy," Serenity shrieked. She froze, her green eyes growing bigger.

I rolled. The belt buckle clanged on the floor. "Run."

Jake swore.

I used his moment of pause and scrambled to Serenity, pushing her toward the door. The belt cracked behind. After snagging our boots and coats, I wrenched open the front door and snatched Serenity's hand. Together, we darted outside.

Down the street we ran. When it appeared Jake wasn't following, I helped Serenity put on her boots and jacket. She put on her hat and mittens while I shrugged into my boots and jacket. I shivered. That was too close. This was a new side of Jake.

"Mommy, can we go to the libwawy?"

It'd be a warm place until Jake left. I hoped Grace didn't suspect why we visited the library a lot, but scarcely checked out books.

Serenity tugged on my coat. "Ple-e-ease?"

"Okay but remember to be quiet in the library."

Serenity skipped ahead and scaled the snowbanks on either side of the sidewalks, stopping just before the street. When I reached the intersection, she had squeezed the snow into a ball. She grinned and tilted her arm back. The snowball pelted the sidewalk and split into smaller pieces.

The action resembled how I felt each time Jake struck. "Come on, we're almost at the library."

Serenity took my hand as we crossed the street to our sanctuary away from Jake.

An old, red truck turned onto the street and parked near the curb. Noel waved. He opened the door, slamming it shut. "Hello there, it's Mary and Serenity going to the library."

Serenity giggled. She released her grip and dashed over to Noel, her gaze tipping upward at him.

Noel squatted. "Have you come to see Miss Grace?"

"No-o-o…"

"Did you come to check out books?"

Serenity shook her head. "Come cuz Daddy mad."

Noel didn't respond but made eye contact with me. He rose with a grunt.

"Jake's not feeling well today. Serenity was bouncing off the walls, so I thought we'd go to the library and park to run off her energy," I rattled off with little thought.

"You two can ride with me out to the tree farm, if you'd like," Noel said softly.

"Yeah," Serenity screeched. "I feed horsies."

Noel laughed.

His laughter eased the tension, and I smiled. My hands curved around Serenity's shoulders. "She's horse crazy, like I was at that age. If my grandparents were still alive, I think Serenity and I would ride horses most days."

"You both can ride the Clydes, if you want."

"You all coming inside, or staying outside?" Grace teased.

Serenity bolted for the librarian, who had become our friend. "Miss Gwace."

Noel sidestepped and paused, whispering in my ear, "Did he hurt you?"

Coldness flooded within at what he asked. We had gotten too close, and now Noel suspected. I wanted to be honest, but it was my fault for angering Jake. I should have kept Serenity quiet. Behind, Grace and Serenity chattered.

I swallowed despite there being nothing to swallow. "No, I'm fine."

"I'll get the coffee brewing," Grace said. "Come inside when you're finished, but don't take too long, or Serenity and I will eat all the cookies."

"Cookies," Serenity exclaimed with a fit of giggles. She took Grace's hand, and they disappeared into the library.

I flinched at a touch on my arm.

Noel removed his hand from my arm. "Mary, if you need help, Grace and I are here."

"Everything's fine. Jake just indulged too much last night and is suffering from the effects of it today." I started for the library. "That's all."

"I saw the bruise on your wrist."

"That was from being klutzy." I entered the entryway of the library.

Instead of joining Grace and Serenity in the library, I went downstairs to where the women's bathroom was. After double-checking that the door was locked, I took off my jacket and sweater. I lifted my t-shirt and winced. I stared into the mirror at the welts on my back. Someone knocked.

"Mary?" Grace asked.

"I'll be out in a minute."

"Noel sent me to check on you. Is everything okay?"

I jammed on my sweater and unlocked the door, opening it. "Yes, I needed the restroom."

"Your husband hits you, doesn't he? That's why you were in the bathroom, checking for bruises."

I gaped. Had Noel told her what Serenity said? I stammered, "I... I told you, 'I needed the restroom.'"

"Honey, I've been in your shoes. And you forget, I've helped hundreds like you."

"We're fine," I scoffed and pushed past her. "It was just one time."

Grace said nothing more but followed me upstairs and into the library.

When I slumped into a chair, I clamped my tongue to keep from wincing. Though neither Grace nor Noel said anything more, they exchanged looks with one another that seemed to carry a suggestive meaning. As both peered at me, I bit my tongue. An elephant had grown in the room between us, and I disliked it.

Nine

Serenity pushed the miniature shopping cart alongside my larger one. She fidgeted with the kids' fruit bowl while I compared prices in the produce section. I hated math, but it was necessary for my slim budget. Days of carefree shopping that took an hour versus an entire afternoon scouring the store for the best bargains now seemed like a dream.

I cringed. Jake had added snack items to the shopping list, such as cookies, donuts, and mini cakes— Items I considered a luxury. I leaned against the cart's handle and sucked in a sharp breath. My jacket rubbed against the fresh bruises, providing a reminder of yesterday morning's incident. More would be added to the collection later if I didn't buy what he wanted.

After calculating the remaining balance, I crossed off the snacks. Baking them would be cheaper, and hopefully Jake would forget he had requested the bakery's sweets.

Serenity put a bag of clementines in her shopping cart without asking.

I sighed and scrutinized the list again. At least they were healthier than Jake's snack items, but I couldn't bake them. I scratched off the coffee creamer. Drinking black coffee while my daughter ate clementines was worth the sacrifice.

"He *is not* a dog. He is a guide dog," Nick's distant gruff voice raised.

A female voice responded.

"Serenity, come with me," I ordered.

We abandoned our carts in the produce section and strode the short distance to the front of the grocery store.

At the customer service desk, Nick argued with a cashier while Ford sat on the floor beside him. "Get me your manager."

The woman narrowed her eyes as she dialed the extension number on the phone. Her fingers twirled the phone cord while she waited.

"Nick," Serenity squealed. She skipped the rest of the way to the counter and stopped where Ford sat.

Ford rose, his tail whipping back and forth.

"Hi, Serenity. Where's your mommy?" Nick questioned.

"I'm here."

Other customers gawked at Nick and exchanged whispers with one another. Small children asked in their innocent voices, 'What's wrong with that man?'

Nick was probably the youngest person they'd ever seen blind in our small town. Their treatment of him was perturbing.

"Can I pet Ford?" Serenity asked.

The golden retriever's tongue lolled as he gazed upon his master.

"No. he's busy working right now. You can pet him the next time you come visit."

Noel was nowhere to be seen. "How'd you get here?"

"I got a ride from Noel. Would you mind if I walked with you two while you're shopping?"

The store manager came. Instead of speaking with Nick, he diverted his attention toward me. "I'm sorry, but dogs aren't allowed in the store."

"I'm blind, not stupid. Speak to me about the issue," Nick snapped.

"Excuse me, sir. That sign on those sliding doors… doesn't it say this store welcomes service animals?" I asked.

The woman behind the counter rolled her eyes.

"Um…" The store manager's cheeks flushed. "I guess…"

"And does this dog not look like a service animal?"

"Mary, forget about it."

"Uh… uh…" The store manager dropped his gaze to the floor. He mumbled something.

"Shame—"

"Mary! I don't want to shop here anymore." Nick spoke to Ford, "Door."

Ford stepped forward. He guided Nick through the sliding doors, and they stopped outside in front of the store.

"You guys should be ashamed of yourselves. That man lost his eyesight serving our country, and this is how you repay him— by not allowing his guide dog to be his eyes," I admonished. "Serenity, let's go. I'm no longer shopping here either."

Everyone gaped.

Serenity took my hand and skipped as we exited the grocery store.

The nerve of those people! Nick had grown up here, and they treated him like they didn't know him.

"Is that you, Mary?"

"How'd you know?"

"Serenity likes to skip." Nick sighed. "Don't ever do that again. I can fight my own battles."

"But—"

"Damn it, Mary. I don't need anyone protecting me."

"Fine. I'm sorry." I blinked. He'd never spoken like that to me before. Serenity leapt off the curb while I stepped off. "Next time, I won't defend you against those idiots."

"They're not idiots, just uneducated."

"Bye Ni-i-ick. Bye Ford," Serenity said, glancing over her shoulder.

"Whatever," I muttered as Serenity and I marched across the parking lot. An occasional breeze careened a chill through my jacket. A cold snap had settled across Minnesota, making the wind chills below zero. I couldn't leave Nick and Ford in this weather.

After starting my car, I buckled Serenity in the car seat and covered her with a spare blanket I kept as part of our winter survival kit. I backed from the parking spot. Even if Nick was upset, his stubbornness wouldn't deter me from ordering him into the car.

When I arrived in front of the grocery store, Nick and Ford had shuffled farther from their original spot on the sidewalk. I cranked down the window. "Get in."

"No, I'll walk." Nick and Ford continued walking.

"Damn it, Nick." I rolled the car alongside them and parked, getting out and slamming the door. "It's too cold for you guys to be out here. How do you think Ford feels with his poor feet on that concrete?"

Nick hesitated, his jaw clenching.

People passed by, staring as they prepared their gossipy mouths for later. I was sure Jake would hear the rumor. The scuttlebutt around this town was like playing a bad game of adult telephone.

"Just get in already."

"Fine!" Nick turned and took a step dangerously close to the store's brick post.

I sprinted. "Nick—"

Nick collided into the post before I finished the warning. He said nothing. Blood pooled within scrapes on his hand and across his nose and cheekbone. A sharp sigh came from him.

"Are you okay?" I grabbed a wad of tissues from my coat pocket and started dabbing at the blood on his face.

Nick clasped a hand over mine, stopping me from dabbing. "Stop. Can you help me to the car, please?"

"How should I…?" I peered into his blue eyes. A longing flooded my body at how much I missed him gazing back. This was the first time Nick had asked for help, and I wanted to treat him with respect.

Fingers curled around above my elbow. I flinched when they pushed on a sore spot.

"I'm sorry. Did I hurt you?"

"No. I bumped it last night, so my elbow is tender today."

"You bumped it, or did Jake grab you?"

"Ready?" I took a step forward and led Nick to the passenger side of my SUV. "You know me, I'm klutzy."

"Don't lie to me."

"We're at the passenger door. I'll put Ford in the backseat with Serenity."

While Nick fumbled to find the handle, I opened the back door and ushered Ford inside. The handle creaked, and Nick stooped to get into the SUV.

I resisted the temptation to shut the door for him. Instead, I entered the driver's side and put on my seat belt. "Where do you want me to drive you? I can drop you off wherever Noel's at, or I can drive you home."

"You didn't answer me about Jake."

Serenity babbled in the back seat to Ford, stroking his silky fur.

"I'm not talking about this with you. I've got to drop you off and drive to Orion to get groceries."

A car honked. I checked the side mirror and found they were waiting for us to move. The blinker clicked, and I veered out of the fire lane. By driving to Orion for groceries, it meant I had less money to spend on food. I sighed. I couldn't shop at a store where their signs about welcoming service animals were hypocrites.

"If it's money you're worried about, I'll pay for your gas and groceries," Nick said in a gentle tone.

"Thanks, but I'll manage."

"Mary. Look at me."

"I can't right now. I'm driving," I replied, turning the car onto the street.

"I'm sorry."

What was he sorry for— Jake hitting me, or for what happened at the grocery store? I wanted to ask but refrained for fear of the answer.

Ten

Fresh snow powder decorated the evergreen trees. I maintained a distance behind the snowplow while it cleared the highway and laid down sand. Between the bald tires and the plow, I dared not pass on the slippery highway this morning. Jake had yet to replace the tires.

Serenity hummed along with the radio's Christmas tunes. At times, she made up her own words in the songs.

A faded green truck edged closer in the rear-view mirror until the driver had come into clear view. My fingers gripped the steering wheel. Jake. He finally caught me. I turned onto the road leading to the Christmas tree farm. Jake's pickup rounded the curve, following.

I stopped near the fence, and he parked beside us.

His door slammed shut. Jake left the truck running and stormed around the front of my car.

"Stay here. Mommy has to talk to Daddy," I said to Serenity.

Jake opened my door.

"Hi, Daddy," Serenity said in a bubbly tone. "They gots lots of Chwistmas trees here."

"They do, don't they?" Jake plastered on a toothy smile, one I recognized as him holding a shout inside. He grabbed my arm.

I complied with getting out and jerked at the force with which Jake slammed my driver's door. Thank God we weren't home, or this would be worse. Jake never chanced witnesses to his anger.

He clicked his tongue and shook his head. "I couldn't believe it when Ollie told me my woman was working here."

"Jake—"

"No wife of mine is working. You belong at home raising our babies and keeping house."

"We owe money. Our house is going into foreclosure, and, if we don't start paying the mortgage soon, we won't have anywhere to live."

Jake's hands clenched and unclenched at his side. His voice rose. "You thought you'd earn enough cash and then leave me. Didn't you?"

"*No*, I'm trying to pay our creditors."

Footsteps shuffled along the porch and clomped on the steps. I held my breath as Ford navigated Nick through the partially frozen, slushy driveway. Earlier in the week, warmer temperatures had allowed cars and trucks to create an array of deep ridges in the mud-gravel road. Even with sight, navigating the uneven terrain was dangerous.

Jake snapped, "You—"

"Mary, is everything okay?" Nick asked.

Ford growled.

Jake spun around and gawked at Ford, then at Nick.

I cleared my throat. "Yeah, Jake needed to talk to me about something that couldn't wait."

"Hi, Jake. It's been a long time."

"I heard you were back," Jake replied, still staring.

"I guess. It's pretty hard learning how to be blind without a crash course. Wouldn't recommend it."

"You're blind?"

"Yup, an entire year now."

"Jake, I'll see you tonight?" I asked, hoping to persuade him into leaving. Getting caught working at the tree farm wouldn't delay tonight's thrashing.

"Yeah, I gotta get back to work." Jake kissed my cheek for show, or rather, for sound. "I'll see you tonight, babe."

As Jake opened his truck door, he waved at Serenity. He glared through the window for a moment and then drove toward the highway.

"You okay? He seemed pretty pissed," Nick said.

Ford groaned, as if in agreement. His tail whipped back and forth, increasing in speed while I tended to Serenity.

"A misunderstanding. Where's Noel today?"

"He's taking care of business for me."

"Oh, business?"

"Ni-i-ick," Serenity shouted. She scampered toward him and embraced his legs. "Can we wide the horses today?"

Nick cracked a slow smile. The first one I had seen since our encounter a week ago. He squatted. "I wish I could, honey, but I can't."

"Why?"

"I need someone with me to help me see."

Serenity leaned her forehead against his. "I help you."

"If your mom comes, then maybe … just maybe, we can go on a sleigh ride."

"O-o-oh. Please, Mommy?"

I glanced at the driveway again. What if Jake was watching, or worse, someone told him?

"Yeah. Please, Mary?" Nick mimicked Serenity's tone. His impish grin allowed another glimpse of our past, one I missed. Seeing his old self again was nice.

"Um-m-m." I couldn't do it. Tell them no. The punishment later would be worth the price of reliving a memory. "Sure. I'll get things ready, and we can leave in half an hour."

"You ready the horses, and I'll make the hot chocolate. Serenity can help me."

"Oh, okay."

"My eyes may not work, but I'm still capable in the kitchen."

"Are you now? I expect you to make lunch then after we get back," I teased.

Serenity motioned her head side to side at our banter.

Nick imitated a knife chopping fast. "You're on. Be prepared to be amazed by my chef-like skills."

I chuckled. "Meet you at the barn in fifteen minutes."

Nick and Serenity held hands, with him walking and her skipping while Ford continued his designated job. When Nick stumbled forward, I held back the need to help him.

My stomach fluttered as I took the reins for the Clydesdale. It had been over ten years since I rode the sleigh, but this would be the first time I wielded the reins. Nick always drove the sleigh before. The horses fidgeted, impatient for me to say the word. I exhaled and loosened my grip.

"Don't be nervous. You'll do fine," Nick reassured.

As if Ford agreed, he laid his head against my boots. He had stretched across everyone's feet on the floor of the sleigh and became our built-in portable heater.

The horses started, and the bells jingled. Serenity's eyes widened, and she turned toward me. "Mommy, that's in the song we sing."

I smiled at her wonder. My daughter was loving Christmas as much as Grandma Hazel did. Another vivid childhood memory slipped into my mind— a view of the eight-track tape's "Jingle Bells" label. Grandma would slide the tape into the player and then grin while asking if I wanted ribbon candy.

Serenity squealed, and my past days of wonderment vanished.

I used a fingertip and rubbed the inside corners of my eyes at the small, rectangular box Serenity held. Across the top, golden letters shone the words ribbon candy.

"You still like ribbon candy?" Nick asked.

I whispered, "Where did you find that?"

"A certain Santa we know found them for me. You had mentioned that Serenity reminded you of Grandma Hazel, and I remembered how much she loved ribbon candy. I thought Serenity might like them."

A sniffle escaped. I stifled another one when Serenity pulled the ribbon off and opened the box.

Her finger traced a red and white candy's folded layers. She glanced, waiting for permission. After I gave a nod, she brought the candy to her mouth and sucked on it.

"It's weally good," she mumbled.

"You okay, Mary?"

"Yeah, thank you for the ribbon candy. I haven't had any since that last Christmas with Grandma Hazel."

Serenity pushed the candy onto my lap, and I chose a green and red plaid one.

"You want one?" she held the box near Nick.

Nick bumped the box and sent several pieces of candy over the edge. He muttered something. His fingers skimmed along the box's side until he reached the top and pulled a green and white ribbon. "Thank you, Serenity. What color did I get?"

"Gween and white."

They continued to talk. Serenity described the scenery in a Christmas magical fashion as a child who believed in Santa would. My heart swelled at their interaction. If someone had seen us, they would have assumed we were a family. Jake had failed at being a part of our family.

A muffled laugh came from Nick. He fought to keep the ribbon candy in his mouth, and at last, a lump appeared on his cheek. "Serenity here thinks we should decorate all the trees along the trail."

"She has an idea there. Some color would be pretty hanging in the trees."

Nick jested back.

The heaviness on my shoulders lightened as we continued along in our winter wonderland. Life with Nick before had been easy, one that I missed. In my current life, Jake exploded daily. Today seemed like a ticking bomb for what tonight would bring with Jake, but I didn't care. Serenity deserved a memory like a sleigh ride.

Eleven

The windows rattled upon a sudden gust. Flurries bombarded the air with little visibility underneath the streetlight. I shivered but resisted bumping up the thermostat. An Arctic front had taken the Midwest hostage, and wind chills were at a dangerous all-time low this year.

"Folks, it is getting nasty out there," the announcer blared.

I increased the volume on the radio. Our county had been upgraded to a blizzard warning in addition to the wind chill. It had been a similar night when…

Jake's coat rustled as he stuffed an arm in the sleeve. "I'm heading to Orson's," he grumbled.

"Jake, please."

The radio chattered about the importance of staying put until weather conditions improved. Jake jammed on his green and cream striped beanie. His bloodshot eyes narrowed. "I'll be fine."

"It's whiteout conditions out there. I doubt Orson's is open in weather like this."

"Woman." Jake tightened his hands into fists at his side. He glanced at the floor as if searching for something. When Jake didn't find it, he slammed the closet door open and rummaged through the mess of coats and shoes.

"What are you looking for?"

His almost six-foot figure stomped toward me. "You hid my boots. Didn't you?"

"No-o-o. You left them in the bedroom."

Jake always did after a night of boozing. It had become routine to move his boots by the door after I woke in the mornings. Serenity distracted me this morning.

Jake leaned forward, his nose touching mine. Spit sprayed onto my face. "Go get 'em."

"Mommy," Serenity said. Teeth rattling, she folded her arms against her chest. "I'm cold."

"It's the wind, sweetie. Let's go get you a blankie, and you can snuggle up with it on the couch and watch a movie."

Crack. His palm connected with my cheek, and he raised it to strike again. Jake screamed, his demand piercing my eardrums.

I recoiled as he struck again. A warm, stinging sensation traveled upward from where Jake slapped. I resisted the urge to bring a hand to my cheek.

"Now!" Jake snarled.

I pressed my lips together and gave a nod.

The boots were lying on the bedroom floor from when he had tossed them last night in his drunken state. I took a blanket from our closet for Serenity. A shadow on the floor grew larger and stopped when Jake loomed in the doorway.

"What the hell do you think you're doin'?"

"I-I-I…" I sputtered, unable to believe he had followed.

"You're supposed to be getting *my* boots, not a blanket."

Rather than say anything, I bent forward and grabbed one boot, then the other. I gave them to Jake. When I sidestepped him in the doorway, he dropped his boots and grabbed above my wrist.

"Next time, you *will* put me first." Jake dug his fingers between the two bones in my forearm. "I'm tired of this 'let's put Jake last' business."

Unwanted tears formed with each blink. I clamped my tongue between my teeth to keep them from escaping. Parents were supposed to put their children first. If Jake couldn't handle Serenity getting attention before him, what would he be like after a baby? How long before Jake suspected something?

"Now, pick *them* up." Jake released my arm with a shove.

"Jake," I whispered, "please don't leave."

He raised a hand, and I flinched.

A small gasp came from Serenity. "Daddy! Hitting bad."

Jake glared as he lowered his hand. The muscle along his jaw trembled, and he turned around. "No, sweetie, I was showing Mommy something."

"You hit her." Serenity placed her little hands on her hips. "I saw you."

Jake clenched his jaw again. Though Jake said nothing, he snatched his boots and muttered toward me. "Do something with that brat. If you don't, I will."

He tromped to the front door and jammed on his boots. When the door opened, snowflakes and a gust blew inside. "I'll see you later," Jake said, and slammed the door.

The tension seeped from my shoulders. Yet, a small part argued we'd be punished later whenever Jake returned. I kneeled and wrapped the blanket around Serenity. "Here you go, sweetie. Why don't you go find a movie, and I'll make popcorn?"

"With hot chocolate?" Serenity grinned.

"You are a chocolate fiend," I teased. "Just like me."

An engine revved outside.

Serenity scampered to the TV stand while I went to the kitchen window. Outside, headlights backed out of the driveway and onto the street. The snow accumulation was difficult to guess since the blizzard had begun midafternoon.

I gathered the dirty dishes and brought them to the sink with a sigh. At least Jake had come home for supper. Yet I almost preferred him gone, like most days when he stayed at Orson's until closing.

Something jingled. I mumbled, rolling over and turning on the lamp beside my bed. The cellphone's tune continued screaming until I answered. I squinted at the alarm clock. It was past last call at the bar. Only one person would call at this hour.

"Mary? It's Orson calling." He quieted.

Jake yelled a string of incomprehensible words in the background. Someone shushed him.

When Jake quieted, Orson spoke again. "Do you want to come get Jake, or should I call one of the police officers?"

"Um…"

The wind howled its warning. My heart pounded at driving in the terrible weather conditions that included whiteouts. I hadn't driven in a blizzard since high school. If I didn't get Jake, he would get angrier.

"Hello?" Orson's voice crackled.

"Can't… can't he stay with you?" I whispered.

It was Orson's fault for continuing to serve Jake past his inebriated state. Orson had no idea what Jake did.

"Jake's a paying customer, not my friend. I have a family to worry about, and, if I bring customers home, I won't hear the end of it from the missus."

I sighed. "Let me wake Serenity, and we'll be on our way."

"Be careful. The wind's picked up since earlier this evening."

The phone beeped, and I found that the call had dropped. I lay the emergency cellphone on the bedside table. The storm's icy grip had wheedled a slow hold inside our home. As the warmth of the bed stayed behind, I shivered in the igloo we seemed to have inhabited.

When I opened the front door, an avalanche of snow toppled onto the entryway rug. The wind howled its occasional scream. I tugged my coat hood over my stocking cap and dashed to the car between gusts. The driver's door clanked.

The wind swayed the car as I fumbled with the keys. My teeth chattered, and I dropped the keys. I removed my glove and groped around on the floor, finding the keys underneath my seat. The engine screeched like an air-raid siren.

I cranked the knob and put the heat on high, waiting for the SUV to warm before I brought Serenity out. The snow danced across the small drift on my windshield. A gasp caused a coughing spell. I couldn't do this.

Tears welled as I fought to regain control of my breathing. "Mom and Dad, I'm so sorry for that night," I whispered.

The engine continued its whine. I had no choice but to get Jake, or we would pay the price whenever he got home. A feeling nagged that we shouldn't go. I held onto the door as the wind threatened to snatch it from my grip and fought with shutting it.

Serenity lolled while I dressed her in winter gear and blankets. At the first gust, she shuddered.

"I'm cold," she mumbled, burrowing closer against me.

I hiked my daughter farther up my shoulder and held her with one arm. Holding her and opening the car door was harder than I remembered. I stared at her car seat. Serenity would have to be unbundled to fit into it and buckled properly. If it would have been possible, my heart sunk to my feet at what I was doing.

Our child deserved to be put first, and that meant her safety. I turned around and used my body to slam the car door shut. Orson or the police could deal with Jake.

Twelve

Chattering teeth and an occasional mumble woke me. Outside, an eerie quietness had fallen, as if last night's blizzard never happened. I exhaled, and a smoky cloud came from my mouth. The storm may have stopped, but the bitter cold remained unyielding and determined to claim our house as a victim. Serenity snuggled closer.

What time was it? I gasped at the time listed on my alarm clock and blinked. After eight, and Jake wasn't home?

I gritted my teeth and slid from underneath the blankets. The house seemed colder this morning than last night when the wind was blowing. After I added more layers over my pajamas, I checked the thermostat. Fifty degrees! The last I had checked, the thermostat was set for sixty-seven.

"Oh… no… we're out of fuel oil," I groaned softly.

"Mommy?" Serenity's teeth clicked together. "It cold."

I stood in the doorway of my bedroom. "Stay under the blankets, honey. I'll get you clothes and try to warm up the house."

"And hot chocolate?" Serenity asked, her green eyes twinkling as she smiled.

"Sure, you can have hot chocolate this morning."

I rooted through Serenity's dresser drawers and closet, gathering her warmest clothing. They were small because of another growth spurt but would do for now until someone refilled our fuel oil tank. Before returning to my bedroom, I turned on the oven and cracked its door open for heat.

When I entered the bedroom, I discovered Serenity crying. "What's wrong?"

"I wet."

"Don't worry, I brought you clean panties."

"I...I want a bath," she sobbed.

"It's too cold right now. Mommy has to call someone to fix the heat, and then you can take a bath."

She continued bawling, and I wanted to join in too.

The bed slumped under my weight. I stroked along Serenity's hairline and onto her cheek. "Let's get you out of your wet pants, huh?"

"Okay," she sniffled.

"You want me to help, or can you do it yourself?"

"I do it."

I laid her clothes on the bed and took the cellphone off the nightstand. "You get dressed. If you need help, I'll be in the kitchen."

Serenity didn't respond but gave a nod. The blankets rustled as she pushed them away.

In the kitchen, I searched through the phone book for the number of the fuel oil company Jake had used last. They probably hadn't been paid like everything else. As the line rang, my stomach roiled. If they refused service, where would Serenity and I go for warmth?

Nick's. His name whispered inside my mind.

"Spruce Point Oil and Propane," a woman answered.

"Hi, this is Mary Edwards. I'm calling because we ran out of fuel oil during the night, and I'm wondering if you can send someone a-s-a-p to refill our tank."

"Who is the account under?"

"My husband, Jake Edwards."

A keyboard clacked. The woman muttered Jake's name several times." Hmm … I'm sorry, but the account is overdue. We can't refill until the bill is paid in full and request that future refills be paid up front."

"Please," I pleaded. "The temperatures are dangerous, and I have a three-year-old daughter to think about."

"I'm sorry, but that's our policy."

"We don't have the money to pay all that right now."

"Have you considered stopping at social services and applying for heating assistance?"

Jake would never let that happen. I sighed. "Thanks anyway, for your help. I'll figure something out."

"You have a good day now."

I shivered. We couldn't stay here with the house temperature dropping. Nick's name haunted me again. The library was closed, and I didn't know where Grace lived.

Our cellphone jingled, and Orson's name flashed across the lit screen. I didn't answer.

"I'm weady for hot chocolate," Serenity sang.

"How about we go to the tree farm?"

"Yeah and see Nick and Ford and Noel!"

I took her hand. "Let's go pack a bag before we go."

"Daddy come too?"

"No, Daddy's at Orson's."

"Oh." Serenity paused. "We get hot chocolate at the tree farm?"

A laugh rumbled from my chest. I ruffled her hair, and we went into her bedroom to pack.

I loosened my grip on the steering wheel as Nick's house came into view. Though his cousin, Christian, inherited the house after his parents died, Nick and his brother had also grown up in this second home. The tree farm had served as a hub for the Hunt family in the past.

Noel's truck was in front of the house.

"Hey, Noel," I mumbled to myself. "Our furnace died, and I wondered if we could stay here until it gets fixed."

As I worked out what to say, it occurred to me that money was needed to 'fix' the problem. Money, we didn't have, because Jake drank it. My fingers ached from clenching the steering wheel again. I clamped my tongue between my teeth to keep from crying. Perhaps I should have waited for Jake.

"Mommy, you think I take a bath here?" Serenity asked, peering back in the rear-view mirror.

No, this was the right decision. I smiled for reassurance. "Maybe. You stay here while I go see if anybody's home."

The tips of Serenity's mittens peeked through the edges of the blanket. She pulled the blanket tighter and glanced at the frosted window toward the horses.

The car still running, I dashed up the porch steps and quickly rapped several times.

Noel answered the door. "Mary, is everything all right?"

"Is it okay if Serenity and I stay for a few hours?"

"You're always welcome here." Noel reached into the closet and put on his jacket. "I'll help you unload Serenity."

Noel said nothing more when we walked to my SUV. He opened the backdoor where Serenity sat.

Serenity greeted him with a shiver.

While Noel tended to my daughter, I shut off the SUV and got our bags. Inside the house, Noel had brought Serenity near the fireplace. Rather than taking off the blankets and her coat, Noel left Serenity and hung his jacket in the closet. "I'll make hot chocolate. That should warm her stomach."

My burning cheeks burned hotter. "We haven't had breakfast yet."

"You girls like pancakes?"

"Pancakes will be fine. I can cook us breakfast, if you'd like."

Noel winked. "Let me, you and Serenity relax by the fire. There's a newspaper on the end table beside the chair if you'd like something to read."

I gaped. The last man who had cooked for me was Grandpa Bill. In our marriage of five years, Jake never cooked and insisted it was a woman's place to be in the kitchen.

The clock's chime caused me to jerk.

"Did something happen this morning?"

I shook my head. "Ran out of fuel oil is all. May I uh… borrow the telephone to make some calls?"

Noel pulled a cellphone from his shirt pocket and extended it. "You need the phone book?"

"Please." I took the flip phone from him. "Mind if I use one of the empty bedrooms upstairs?"

"Sure. Serenity can keep me company in the kitchen, and I might teach her how to make animals out of pancakes."

Serenity glanced at us, her eyes widening. "You make animals out of pancakes?"

"Of course, I thought all little girls like to eat animal pancakes?" Noel teased.

I slipped away during their banter and retrieved the phonebook from the kitchen. Surely, I could find a place that would refill our tank. Not wanting anyone to hear, I tiptoed upstairs and along the hallway when a floorboard creaked.

"Hello?" Nick asked.

My shoulders drooped. "It's only me."

"Mary, what are you doing here? I thought you had today off?"

"I did— I mean I do. We ran out of fuel oil, so I brought Serenity here until I can find someone to refill our tank."

"Where's Jake?"

"Um…"

"He didn't come home?" Nick pressed a button on a machine that resembled a tape player and removed the headphone dangling around his neck, setting them aside. He rose from his chair. "Is he okay?"

"I'm assuming he slept at Orson's. What is that machine?"

"Books on tape. It's about all I can do around here." Nick chuckled drily.

"Nick Hunt, quit feeling sorry for yourself. You might not see, but you have a brain in that head of yours. Use it!"

"You don't know what it's like."

"I don't have time to deal with this. Right now, my three-year-old daughter needs a heated house, so she doesn't freeze to death in this weather." I whirled around and stormed into an empty guest bedroom.

"Call Spruce Point Oil and Propane."

"I already did, and they won't because Jake didn't pay—" I cut off the rest of the sentence that had vomited from my mouth.

"I'll loan you the money."

"No, Jake will find out."

"He's going to after I have a chat with him about taking care of you and Serenity."

I stepped back out into the hallway. "Please don't. You'll make things worse."

"You don't deserve what he's doing to you."

I stiffened. Even if I applied for heating assistance, the application would likely take a few days before we could get fuel oil. We needed heat now. I sighed, knowing Jake would find out one way or another. His spies reported everything. "Fine, you can loan me the money. Consider it as my advanced paycheck."

Thirteen

I gripped and loosened my grip on the steering wheel several times as the car idled in the parking lot of social services. The Spruce Point Oil and Propane receptionist's words repeated themselves. Yesterday couldn't happen again.

A woman peered through the window.

Jake would freak if he learned I was here. I still hadn't told him about the fuel oil running out. It would only bring up the question of 'how did you get it filled?'

The same woman, who peered through the window, exited the building. Her arms were crossed as if she were keeping her jacket closed. She knocked on my window. When I opened the car door, she spoke. "Why don't you come in? You've been here a while."

I moistened my lips and swallowed. "Let me get my daughter first, and we'll be in."

"I'll wait for you."

Serenity had already unbuckled herself by the time I opened her door. She skipped around the front of the car. "Hi," she said, stopping her skip. "What's your name?"

"April. What's yours?" the woman responded with a smile.

My daughter showed four fingers. "Serenity. I'm four."

"Oh my. Have you seen Santa yet?"

"She turns four at the end of January." I placed a hand on Serenity's upper back and urged her to move toward the social services entrance.

"I see Santa almost every day." Serenity continued talking about Christmas as we meandered into the building. She paused near the receptionist's desk. After a quick glance at the waiting area, she whispered, "Don't tell anyone, but Noel is Santa Claus. He tolds me so."

"I promise to keep your secret," April responded in a hushed tone.

"Serenity, we better let this nice lady get back to work," I said, prepared to speak with the receptionist.

"Actually, I can help you. You can follow me to my office down the hall here." April gestured toward the hallway and smiled at Serenity. "And I even have a Christmas tree in my office that comes with presents for little girls just like you."

Serenity squealed.

True to her promise, April allowed Serenity to choose one present under the small Christmas tree that sat in the corner of her office. While my daughter unwrapped her present, April asked, "How can I help you?"

"Mary Edwards." I shook her hand. "Um… someone suggested I should apply for heating assistance after we ran out of fuel oil yesterday."

April removed her coat and hung it. "Are you without heat?"

"A friend paid for our fuel oil refill. I'm not sure what we would have done otherwise since…" My gaze wandered to Serenity pulling a small figurine from the box. "…money's tight."

"Are you single, divorced, or married?"

"Married."

"Where does your spouse work?" April sat in her office chair and jotted something on a notepad.

Serenity babbled to herself as she played with the figurine.

I slumped into the chair in front of April's desk. "Jake works at the lumber mill."

"I assume you don't?"

"Mommy works for Nick and Ford and Noel."

"I just started part-time at Hunt's Tree Farm. Nick Hunt and his guide dog have returned to the area after serving overseas."

"Uh-huh, and who is this Noel?"

"I guess you could say he's a caretaker."

April nodded. Her pen scratched across the paper, leaving behind curly loops. When she finished, the pen and notepad were pushed aside. A drawer slid, and she thumbed through the papers within. "I suspect you probably qualify for more than just heating assistance."

"Oh, my husband won't like that. He's already going to be upset with me for being here."

"Why?" April placed a small stack of papers on her desk. "We have quite a few families who are on assistance with a spouse that works at the mill."

"That's how Jake is."

"I think you would qualify for food stamps, heating assistance, and possibly medical assistance. Of course, that's dependent upon what Jake makes at the mill."

"I… I don't know…"

April lifted the applications and extended them. "Take these applications home and look them over. If you decide to apply, call me or stop by."

"Thanks." I turned toward Serenity. "What do you say for your present?"

"Tank you," Serenity said with a grin, holding a miniature Santa. She cradled the figurine and rose from the floor.

"You ready to go?"

"Bye-e-e." Serenity waved as I opened the office door.

We ambled through the hallway and entered the waiting room when Grace spoke. "Mary?"

"Miss Gwace," Serenity exclaimed. She dashed ahead and hugged the elderly librarian.

I rolled the papers and fidgeted with them. Of all people we might run into in the waiting room. It had to be Grace. Was my visit here confidential? I swallowed at the possibility that April or the receptionist would say something about us being here to other people.

"Mary, is everything okay?" Grace asked.

"What are you doing here?"

"I stop in and visit with the Abuse Network workers a couple times a week."

"Oh."

"Look what Apwil gave me." Serenity raised the Santa figurine.

"That was nice of her. You know who he reminds me of?" Grace teased.

My daughter giggled. "Noel."

I placed a hand on Serenity's shoulder. "We need to get going. Daddy will be home soon and will want supper."

Grace glanced at the clock but didn't mention my excuse about supper. She shifted her gaze back to me. "I hope you and Serenity stop at the library tomorrow."

"You bwing more cupcakes?"

I ignored my daughter's question. "We'll try. Serenity, let's go."

Out in the car, I started it and closed my eyes. Grace wanted an acknowledgment out loud of what Jake did to us. She knew. Noel knew. Everyone did, but I made the topic become the unicorn in the room. No amount of the creature's magic would hide the clues I sought to deflect from.

"Mommy? Why you lie?"

A lump engorged itself in my throat at the truth in her question. I swallowed. "What do you mean?"

"Daddy says you lie."

I rubbed my watering eyes, making the stinging sensation worse. Jake was right. I had grown into a liar.

I stared at the requirements for the heating assistance application. Proof of income? Jake never brought his pay stubs home. If I called the mill's human resources inquiring about them, Jake would find out and demand answers.

The oven timer buzzed, and I removed the tater-tot hot-dish onto the stove. As I passed the kitchen window,

Jake's green pickup pulled into the driveway. I dashed to the table and gathered the applications, hiding them under our overdue bills on the kitchen counter. "Serenity, Daddy's home. Time to come to the table and eat."

Serenity shut off the TV and darted to the table per our routine every night.

I was wiping the table when Jake entered. He hung his jacket and took off his boots without saying a word.

"We're having tater-tot hot-dish for supper tonight," I said upon my return to set the table.

"Sounds good," he replied.

"How was work?"

"It went, I guess." Jake shrugged. He glanced at Serenity with a smirk. "I left a present for you in the truck. After supper, I'll go get it for ya."

"What is it?" Serenity asked, her eyes widening.

Jake chuckled.

I placed the tater-tot hot-dish in front of Jake and waited for him to dish up first. "Did you want me to butter a dinner roll?"

"Please."

While he served himself, I sliced three dinner rolls and started buttering them. I stifled my shock when he took Serenity's plate. It had been a long time since Jake helped Serenity with anything.

"You want cheese on it?" Jake rattled the shredded cheese bag.

Serenity glanced at me, then nodded.

As we ate, I couldn't help sneaking glances at Jake. Something happened today. An ache grew the longer Jake acted like when we dated, and it was enough to reignite hope.

"Did you have plans for tonight?" Jake met my gaze. "I was thinking after Serenity opens her present, we could use it."

I tipped my head to the side.

Jake grinned.

My heart wrestled in two pieces. Half said to be wary while the other believed in this demeanor.

"Daddy? Why'd you get me present?"

"When I was at the store, it made me think of the other day when we put up the Christmas tree."

I sucked in water, and a coughing fit refused to subside. Please don't say you bought brand new ornaments for the tree. Between him and Serenity, they would be broken soon.

Jake frowned. "You okay?"

"Swallowed wrong," I wheezed, erupting in another coughing spell.

"We decowate the tree?"

"Yeah, we'll decorate the tree tonight."

I blinked and studied my hot dish on the plate. Why couldn't there be more moments like this with Jake? If he stayed this way, at least our life would be happier. A voice inside whispered the beast within would strike again by the end of the evening.

Fourteen

I sighed at the muddy footprints leading from the front door to our bedroom. The linoleum flooring had become subjected to the abuse of gritty sand stuck on the bottoms of Jake's boots in the five years we lived here. As I stared at the worn floor, it related to the pattern of my life. No matter how hard I scrubbed, the floor kept its scars. I opened the cupboard underneath the sink and glanced toward the bedroom, where Jake still slept.

If he didn't wake soon, it would be another unpaid workday. The water drummed against the bucket as it filled. "Should I wake Jake up?" I questioned under my breath.

Jake seemed to miss work more and more. The stack of bills on the countertop told of angry tales with its large, bold 'payment overdue.' Each day another overdue bill came in the mail, or a collection agency left a message on our voicemail. Yesterday's foreclosure notice rested on top of the paper stack. He had to be woken.

I shut off the water and added two capfuls of cleaning solution into the bucket. Sentences jumbled inside my head as I worked out what to say. Footsteps shuffled across the floor, and I stiffened.

Jake was awake.

"Morning," Jake grumbled, rubbing his bloodshot eyes. He removed the empty coffeepot and stood with it, waiting. "You done with the sink?"

I gaped.

Jake smiled. "What?"

"Nothing," I muttered and lifted the bucket onto the counter.

"Thanks." Jake turned on the water and filled the coffeepot. While the coffee brewed, he embraced me from behind and kissed my cheek.

My lips fidgeted, and I closed my eyes. I braced myself against what he had planned next. Prior experience had taught me not to mistake his affection without a motive.

Jake rested his jaw on my shoulder, his hands sliding downward and stopping between my hips. "Do you feel anything yet?" he asked softly.

I fought the shiver within that threatened to expose my secret. The coffeepot sputtered at the end of its cycle, and I wriggled loose from his embrace. I took a clean cup off the drying rack. "It's too early."

"When are you supposed to get … you know?"

"Maybe in a week, week and a half? I'd have to look at a calendar to know for certain."

Jake frowned. "That long?"

"Why don't you get ready for work, and I'll get your coffee ready."

"Better make it to go." Jake scurried to the bathroom and shut the door. A second later, water roared from the tub faucet, then the shower started.

I placed the clean cup into the cupboard and retrieved a travel mug. When I finished with his coffee, I carried the bucket of water and set it beside the muddy tracks. The shower still running, I began mopping the floor.

With each dunk, the water in the bucket turned into a darker gray color. The shower shut off. I hauled the bucket to the sink and emptied it. The usual noise of drawers sliding open and shut after Jake's shower seemed louder this morning with each bang. His mood had soured about something.

A door thumped against the wall. I swished out the sediment at the bottom of the bucket. The rest of the floor would have to wait until Jake left. I backed away from the sink and whirled around when the same muddy boots stomped across the floor.

"What the hell is this?" Jake hurled something. "I asked you earlier about being pregnant yet, and you lied to me."

I flinched. The dispenser bounced off my shoulder and onto the floor. A circular disc rolled to a stop and wobbled before landing upside down.

No-o-o... Don't tell me...

My body drooped. The birth control pills lay there, revealing a secret I had worked hard to keep. In my distraction with Serenity being hungry and with Jake's muddy footprints, I had forgotten to hide the evidence.

Jake grabbed the back of my neck and pushed me toward the floor. "Look at it," he shouted. "What is it?"

"B-b-birth control."

"Pick it up."

"You're hurting me." I clawed at the noose.

Jake shook, his fingers clenching tighter with each shake. "I said, 'pick it up!'"

I swallowed and grasped the dispenser, the pills rattling inside the palm of my hand. "Please," I pleaded. "I'm sorry."

Jake gave a shove.

I staggered. My feet tripped over each other. I fell forward, groping for anything to break my fall. A fiery jolt flew up my left arm.

"Mommy," Serenity screamed. Footsteps slapped against the floor from the living room.

A slap against skin cracked. "Go to your room."

"No…" I whispered, turning my head.

Serenity whimpered. She cowered as Jake advanced toward her with a raised hand.

"Leave her alone." I scrambled to my feet and lunged at him, connecting with his chest.

Jake stumbled a few steps.

Before he could recover, I leapt again and flailed against anything I could. "Leave her alone!"

Jake grabbed my left arm, twisting it as I continued striking him with my free hand and kicking his legs. A loud crunch shattered the air. He dropped my arm, and it swung like a pendulum.

I screamed.

A fist connected with my eye. I teetered and tried to raise my broken arm, but it just dangled there. Another fist swung toward my face, and I moved my other arm to intercept it. I groaned as the force of his blow struck.

Jake continued pummeling, and soon I crumpled to the floor. He delivered a last kick.

"You're done taking these!" Jake snatched the birth control pack from the floor and marched to the sink. One by one, the pills clinked. The water turned on, and the garbage disposal ground.

I fumbled into an upright position by using a chair. "Jake, please. We can't afford a baby."

Jake spun around.

I staggered for the front door, but wasn't fast enough, and my head collided against a wall. Decorations crashed to the floor. A fistful of my hair went taut, and Jake pulled until I peered into his narrowed eyes.

"You just don't worry about that!"

Tears welled and stung like the clinking pills.

Jake gave my hair another jerk and led me toward the table like an uncooperative dog. "I'll show you right now."

Serenity had crouched under the table. Her little eyes widened.

"Let me go." I dragged my feet.

Jake tugged at my scalp. "You'll do as I say!"

"Stop it."

We stopped at the table, where Jake groped at the front of my pants while still holding onto my hair. The jeans unfastened, Jake contorted my body until I faced the table.

I squirmed and scratched at him. "Stop it!"

Jake continued to hold my hair hostage and jabbed an elbow in my back, forcing me to bend over the table.

Oh God, please don't do this. A sob broke through.

"No, no, no," I screamed.

A long rip loosened my pants. My exposed skin prickled under the cool air, and I writhed against the table's edge. Not with Serenity in the room.

The captive hand lifted, and I kicked, connecting a foot against his stomach.

Jake swore.

I pressed off the table and stumbled past Jake, but he snagged my waist.

"Cover your ears," I warned Serenity.

I flailed as Jake turned us toward the table. He swore, tightening his grip and then slamming my head against the edge of the table. A white-hot light slashed across my skull. Black spots swirled around in my periphery. Darkness descended.

I moaned. My arm…

Garbled voices, clunking sounds followed, and footsteps hastened across the floor.

Serenity…

A small hand shook me. "Mommy."

Where's Jake?

A woman talking in the background.

Grace?

Cascading, sharp pain rippled across my skull as if someone had swung a sledgehammer against my head. I whimpered. The shaking stopped. A child, my child, was crying nearby. I reached for her, but my arm remained in its sprawled position.

"M--a--r-y." A woman's voice stretched in slow-mo time.

How had she gotten here? My eyelids fluttered. The bright shimmer produced lightning bolts, and I squinted at the blur. I shivered. Cold.

"Help…" The rest of Grace's sentence faded.

Cement must have replaced my body. Heaviness had settled over me, and it was unlike anything I had experienced before. I willed for something to move.

Grace consoled Serenity.

I took shallow breaths. I wanted to scream until my throat became raw. What time was it?

Large hands braced my head, and something stiff brushed against my chin. I recoiled. "Don't."

A man responded.

I don't know what he said, but his tone was soothing. "One. Two. Three." The voice counted.

They lifted me onto a hard surface, and I winced.

"N-n-no," I rasped.

Grace spoke. Her soft, silky hand squeezed my good one.

Tears wriggled through my cracked eyelids and slid onto my cheeks.

Someone draped a blanket over me. The wheels on the gurney rattled as the strangers rolled it along. Cold air hit my face, causing me to gasp. Again, someone counted to three. They lifted and pushed my carriage forward into the ambulance, where it blocked the wind.

"Mommy." A shrill shriek rose above the noise.

"Ser—"

A door slammed, startling me. The ambulance's sirens pierced through the throb in my head. Jake! My muscles tensed.

The same male voice talked, comforting me.

Safe. I allowed myself to relax.

Pressure exerted itself upward on my eyelid. A blinding light whisked around. Where was I? Through the blurriness, a woman's face hovered above mine. Was I at the hospital? My hand jerked as something pierced the skin.

The pain subsided. Blackness settled upon me once again.

Fifteen

Wheels clattered. A frigid gust slapped my face, and I awoke from what seemed like the bottom of a well. Voices conversed, but a haze shrouded their identities. I tried to sit upright. The voices chattered faster, and hands prevented me from rising.

Bright lights and shadows swirled above. A door slid open and shut, and the wheels' tune changed. Memories of riding Cotton faded in and out as I floated across the air onto a board. The voices continued, like they came from afar. A flashlight shone in one eye then flicked to the other.

I shivered. Something metal skimmed across my skin in an upward motion, and my clothes loosened. A moan hissed. Had it come from me?

Faint laughter glided over a green pasture on a warm and sunny day. That laughter… it had been years since I heard them. "Mom." I cupped my hands around my mouth and shouted, "Dad."

Only laughter responded.

I stiffened. Was I dead? Something clanged that did not come from in here. If I could hear that, it meant I wasn't dead.

Sneakers squeaked against a floor. Fingers brushed along my chest, pressing on sticky circles. A snap clicked, and the bed jerked forward. Doors banged.

My head throbbed in sync with each pounding heartbeat. Would I never stop flying?

More laughter carried on the soft breeze. Barbed wire fence lined the perimeter of the pasture to my grandparents' ranch. This day seemed familiar, but I couldn't remember why.

You were happy, free from guilt.

"Mary, can you open your eyes?" a woman asked near my ear. I should have recognized her voice but couldn't recall the doctor's name.

"Hurt," I rasped.

"We're gonna take care of you."

"Jake."

"Is that who did this to you?"

"Ser-serenity."

"Your daughter's fine and is being cared for by your friend. We're going to do a CT scan to check for brain bleeding and your eye then do x-rays on your arm," the woman replied.

Horses frolicked with one another while others grazed. I followed the laugher. Along the fence line, Grandma Hazel blew bubbles while a young child and my mom chased after the floating iridescent circles. My dad and grandpa lazed on a blanket with two others, their backs facing me.

I crept closer, trying to catch a glimpse of the unknown couple's faces. *You know who they are…*

A lump lodged itself in my throat, and I blinked. The tears collected on my eyelashes. This day never happened. The couple was me and Nick, and this day had been a future dream.

"Mary, stay with us." The same woman interrupted me from the movie of what never was.

Someone dabbed my face with a cloth. The tears that had fallen in my dream were also real and trailing through caked blood. Someone would say it's from the pain. Perhaps it was, or it was being able to see a glimpse of our lives, if death hadn't snatched *him*.

My eyes fluttered open, and I gasped. Serenity. I had to get her out of here before Jake came back. Blurriness wobbled like I was underneath water. Nausea wavered, threatening to upturn the bile in my stomach. I gagged. An acrid taste remained in my mouth.

Someone brought a straw to my dry lips. "Take a drink of water, honey. It'll help."

"G-g-grace?" I rasped. Why was she here? Where was I? My heart pumped faster. Had she heard what Jake did? I vomited.

The elderly librarian, who had become my friend, took a tissue and wiped around my mouth. "Serenity is with Noel and Nick."

Tears leaked, and a lump wedged itself in my throat. I blinked. The blurriness diminished until Grace came into clear view. She continued cleaning my mess.

I stuck out the tip of my tongue to wet my lips, but nothing happened.

Grace threw the tissues in the garbage and washed her hands. "I was so scared when little Serenity came alone to the library."

After she had dried her hands, Grace lifted the water glass, and I sucked the straw she offered. Cold water reprieved the desert state of my mouth and throat. She pulled it away before I finished.

"M-m-more." My voice cracked.

"You're gonna get sick, if you gulp it down too fast." Grace set the glass on the bedside table and took my hand. She whispered, "I've never prayed so hard for someone to be all right."

"She got you?"

"Poor thing had run to the library without a coat and said—" Grace's face contorted as she fought the glistening tears. "'Mommy won't wake up.'"

"I'm sorry." I shifted positions on the bed and winced. The brief movement intensified the throb inside my head. I swallowed. "Did she... did she see..."

"I don't think so. Serenity said she closed her eyes and covered her ears like you told her to."

"It's my fault. Jake found my birth control pills." I paused and closed my eyes. "I should have gone along and gotten pregnant like he wanted."

"Oh, honey. He still wouldn't change even if you had."

Someone cleared their throat. Rubber squeaked on the floor, and a male officer rounded the corner of the bed. He silenced the radio chatter. "I'm Officer Cody

Benjamin. Could you tell me what happened that led you to the hospital?"

The room became warm. Had he been here the whole time? I forced a swallow past the building pressure in my throat. His hazel eyes stared back.

"Ma'am." His tone softened. "We know your husband did this."

The pain intensified in my head, and the tears did nothing for relief. I whimpered.

"Mary," Grace said.

"Has your husband done this before?"

"No." Why was I lying? They knew.

"So, he became upset upon finding your birth control pills?"

Officer Benjamin *had* overheard what I said to Grace. I avoided his gaze and murmured, "Yeah."

The pen scribbled across his notepad. Officer Benjamin gave a quick peek at me and continued writing. "I've worked fifteen years on the job, and I've seen more domestic abuse than I care for. Please, let us help you."

"Mary, think of your daughter," Grace pleaded.

Snot dribbled onto my lips. The clog in my throat swelled, and I wheezed. Air. I gripped the bedrail. "I-I-I can't breathe."

The machine screamed. A nurse raced into the room and placed an oxygen mask over my mouth and nose. "You're upsetting my patient. Get out."

Officer Benjamin shoved the pen and notepad in his coat pocket. He left without another word.

Grace followed him into the hallway, and they talked. She shook a finger at him.

"Easy, just take a breath," the nurse encouraged.

"Grace, I need her statement. It'll make it more compelling for the charges against him." Officer Benjamin raised his voice. "That Jake has been abusing her for years and getting away with it."

"You know better than to bully a victim."

"People talk and they aren't an exception. I'll submit the information of what I have. But I'm telling you, her statement will strengthen the case against him." Officer Benjamin stormed out of view.

"Your breathing is better," the nurse said as she studied the monitor's screen. She removed the oxygen mask. "How are you doing on pain?"

"I'm fine," I mumbled.

Grace entered and gave me a smile. "I'm sorry. Cody means well, but he doesn't have the subtle tact needed in abuse cases."

"If you don't need anything else, I need to do my rounds," the nurse said.

I thanked her. When she exited my hospital room, I met Grace's gray eyes. "Is Noel bringing Serenity?"

"Not until tomorrow. Dr. Sasha wanted you to rest before seeing her and suggested calling so Serenity knows you're okay."

"How… how long do I have to stay?"

"I'm not sure. Your arm needs surgery yet."

"Do you have a mirror?"

Grace nodded. She turned toward her purse resting on a chair and opened it, withdrawing a compact. The compact unsnapped with a soft click. "You need to leave him."

I didn't respond. The beating wouldn't have been this serious if I hadn't fought him. A voice reminded me of the time he tried to strike Serenity with his belt.

"You ready to look at the damage Jake caused?" Grace asked. She extended the open compact.

In the mirror, a different woman stared back. I dared not touch the deep purple bruises that adorned around my eye and on my forehead. If Jake had done this, what did my daughter look like?

Sixteen

The doctor droned on about the specifics for my upcoming afternoon surgery. Her voice faded to the background as I stared at the doorway, hoping for Serenity's arrival.

A woman dressed in a police uniform peered into my room from the hallway. "May I come in?"

Grace waved.

The petite woman stopped near the foot of the bed. Her brown eyes moved back and forth as she studied me. "Boy, your husband really did a number on you. How you feelin'? Does the doctor need to adjust your pain meds?"

I faked a smile. "I'm fine."

The doctor excused herself and left with the policewoman staring after her.

"A concussion, broken arm, an orbital fracture, and all the bruises you received. And you were raped besides. I doubt you're 'fine.'"

Rape? Could a husband rape a wife?

"The pain is tolerable." My insides squirmed. There was no making up excuses anymore. My injuries screamed abuse. I waited for her to question me about what happened.

"You're lucky your daughter went for help. I'm here to inform you Jake's been arrested and will be in jail until his bond hearing."

"When is that?" Grace asked.

"The Clerk of Court will set it up tomorrow."

"Will the restraining order be in place by then?"

"I didn't apply for a restraining order," I said.

"In cases like this, it's automatically done for your safety," the policewoman responded.

"Oh."

Sleepiness seeped in, and I found it difficult fighting against the sleep my body craved. I needed… what did I need?

The policewoman and Grace chatted more about Jake and what should be done.

Jake was in jail. Someone needed to post bail money to release him. I suspected his folks if Jake called them. They were vacationing in Texas for the winter though. Could bail be made with a money wire?

A new feeling washed over me, one I hadn't felt in a long time. Safe. My eyelids slid closed under the heaviness weighing upon them.

"Mommy." A small hand shook my shoulder. "Wake up."

I winced, mumbling something to the effect of 'don't.' Effort. It took effort prying my eyes open enough to see Noel and Serenity standing at the edge of my bed. Grace sat in the corner near the window.

"Hi." my voice cracked.

"Sorry. She was really worried about you," Noel said.

Serenity laid her head against my shoulder and outstretched her arm across my stomach. I clenched my teeth to keep from saying ow. Her tears soaked into my hospital gown. "You wouldn't—" She hiccupped. "Wake up."

I stroked her tangled hair. How did you tell a three-year-old her daddy almost killed her mommy? A voice whispered that she already knew. Jake had hurt her too. My throat burned. I should have protected her by leaving him earlier. I cradled her closer. "I'm sorry, honey"

Noel slumped into a folding chair. "Where are you staying after your discharge?"

"I… I don't know. All my family has died, and my in-laws are in Texas."

"Nonsense. I consider you the granddaughter I never had," Grace said. "You'll stay with me."

"That would be wise." Nick and his guide dog lurked around the doorway. He fidgeted with Ford's leash, gripping and loosening it. "It'll take Jake longer to find you than if you stayed at the tree farm."

"What about our clothes and my job?"

"After you discharge from the hospital, Noel and I will take you by the house and help you pack a few things," Grace replied.

Noel spoke. "Don't worry about the job. We need you to heal first and decide where you go from here with Jake."

Serenity stirred. Her green eyes met mine. "Mommy, are we moving?"

"Yes, you and I are moving without Daddy." I caressed above her jawline. A fresh mark showed on Serenity's cheek from where Jake had hit her.

Serenity touched it. "Daddy hurt me."

"He hurt me too." I kissed the top of her head. "We're going somewhere he can't hurt us anymore."

I hoped my assurance had convinced Serenity, though it hadn't convinced me. Jake was still my husband. In the last three years, leaving him never strayed far from my mind. I stayed. I stayed for punishment.

"Would Jake look for you at my house?" Grace asked.

"I don't know. Jake has spies around town that report to him about where I'm at, and what I'm doing. That's how he found out about my job at the tree farm."

Noel and Grace exchanged questionable looks with one another. Noel shrugged. "Do you think she'd be safer at the tree farm?"

"It'll be the first place Jake checks," Nick said. "Especially since Mary and I have a history with each other."

He, Noel, and Grace discussed their concerns amongst themselves.

I had underestimated the definition of family. All three considered themselves a part of mine, even Nick.

"I'd like to stay at Grace's," I interjected.

Nick and Ford eased forward. "Someone should stay with you and Serenity when Grace is at work."

"I—"

"Good afternoon—whoa, you sure got a lot of company." A nurse halted beside Nick. "I'm here to prep you for the surgery."

Serenity gawked at her.

"The doctor needs to fix Mommy's arm, but we'll see each other tomorrow," I explained and kissed her goodbye.

"I wanna stay with you," she whined.

"Hey, Serenity. Come over here. Ford has a secret to tell you." Nick relaxed his hand on Ford's back and squatted.

Serenity complied, still mumbling, "I want my mommy."

Ford's tail wagged, and he poked his nose against her hand.

Nick whispered, "Maybe if we ask Noel, he'll take us on another sleigh ride."

A loud gasp came from Serenity. Her hair whipped about as she spun around toward Noel. "With reindeer?"

Noel's rich laugh permeated the room above everyone's, including my own pained one. He pulled a peppermint stick from his pocket. "The Clydesdales might get sad if we borrow Santa's reindeer."

"Is that for me?" Serenity pointed at the peppermint stick.

"How about we leave it here for your mommy? That way, when she misses you, all she has to do is pick it up and think of you." Noel held the peppermint stick out in front of Serenity. "You better give it a kiss first."

Serenity puckered her lips and leaned forward, kissing the peppermint stick. Afterwards, she blew me a kiss. "Bye, Mommy. I love you."

Noel set the peppermint stick on the bedside table and gave a wink. "We'll take good care of your girl."

The nurse waited as Noel and the others exited the room. I finally understood why my daughter believed he was Santa.

Seventeen

As Grace drove farther down the street, the tighter I gripped the door handle. Jake was in jail. I repeated the mantra. My stomach churned. I might barf. Grace parked in front of the house where Jake and I had lived together for five years.

I jerked as she shut off the car.

Grace placed a hand on my thick bandages and spoke in a soothing tone. "It'll be all right, honey. Noel and I are here for you."

A shiver chilled my insides. I swallowed, but there was nothing to swallow. "Let's go."

Noel and Grace followed me inside. I blinked, and the tears dripped off my eyelashes at the rubble left behind. Was this my house? The breath I sucked in ignited into a slow burn.

"We should start packing," Grace said.

"I have to clean." Glass crunched under my shoes as I squatted to pick up the broken glass.

"Leave it."

The pink birth control compact lay in the center of the chaos. I should have remembered to hide them that morning. No… I should have thrown them and gotten pregnant like Jake wanted.

Despite the effort in steadying my fingers, they still shook. Grace took my hand in hers, her gray eyes peering into mine. I sniffled.

"You have to leave him, sweetie."

"I—"

"Think of Serenity. Next time he'll kill you and leave her without a mother."

I licked my chapped lips and whispered, "Jake will never let us go."

"We'll help you," Noel said. "I'll help you pack while Grace packs for Serenity. We need to hurry."

Using Grace's hand for support, I rose from the floor and brushed debris off my jeans. We tiptoed through the wreckage trail. Heaviness crept into my legs the closer we approached the bedrooms.

"S…S… Serenity." I pointed. A fist-sized hole in the door marked my daughter's bedroom.

Disaster had struck the master bedroom too. Dresser drawers laid in multiple pieces with clothes tossed about the room. Blankets and pillows lay strewn. The vanity mirror had large shards broken in a circle of what looked to be another fist.

I lifted a mirror shard and held it. It had been a few days since I last examined the damage to my face. An ugly stream of black, blue, and purple reflected off the mirror. Those same fists had damaged me like our belongings. I dropped the shard, and it shattered into smaller pieces.

Noel dumped a dusty suitcase onto the bed and unzipped it. "Anything you want, toss it in here. I'll go through the clothes."

I fished out undergarments and socks from the wreckage of the dresser drawers while Noel sifted through the tangled clothes on the floor. We worked together in silence.

After what seemed to be a long time, Grace appeared in the doorway. "We need to go. I just got word Jake's on his way home."

Noel zipped the overstuffed suitcase and carried it behind Grace and me. He put my only possessions into the trunk.

I lurched upon the trunk's slam.

Grace shifted the car into drive.

I argued silently between going back and leaving. Serenity's confession that she thought I was dead made the final decision.

We met Jake at the end of the street, and Grace sped up the car.

In the mirror, Jake jumped from the moving car and chased us for a block. When he quit, Jake shook a hand and yelled something.

"Don't forget about the restraining order," Grace said.

"How do I get it dropped?"

Grace continued driving without an answer. On the highway, she pulled the car into somebody's driveway and stared ahead. "Why do you want to go back to him?"

"He's my husband."

"That's not why." Grace's gray eyes bored into mine for a long minute. "Do you think you deserve to be beaten?"

A lump in my throat clogged any ability to reply. I squeezed my eyes shut. The tears came anyway, the ones I had held in for too long.

"O-o-oh, honey." Grace leaned over and embraced as best as she could in a car, holding me as I cried.

"I-I-I…" I sobbed. "… killed my parents."

"No, you didn't," Noel said. "Nick told me your folks died in a car accident when you were in high school."

"I called them to come get me from a friend's house during a blizzard. When they came, I begged them to let me drive because I wanted more practice driving in bad weather."

"Sweetie, anyone driving could have an accident in a blizzard," Grace said.

"It's my fault. I should have stayed at my friend's house." I sniffled.

"Your parents wouldn't want you to punish yourself for their death. They'd want you happy."

"I agree. You have an anxious little girl waiting for your arrival," Noel stated.

Grace wiped my face. "What do you think? Should we go make that darling daughter of yours happy?"

I nodded. They didn't hate me. *You didn't tell them about how you killed him.*

The engine hummed as Grace stepped on the gas pedal and pulled back onto the highway. While she drove, I stared at the passing trees. A part longed for the past where my grandparents and parents surrounded me. I also missed who Jake used to be before this beast consumed him.

"Do you think Jake will get help?" I asked.

"When did he start hitting you?" Grace glanced at me, then at the road again.

"I don't remember. He didn't always drink so heavily."

"You never know. Alcoholics are pretty good at hiding that, especially one as high functioning as your husband."

"I still love him."

The word 'love' seemed like poison when talking about Jake. I did, and I didn't. It was more of a mutual love than a deep love that never fully extinguished.

"Let's focus on your recovery and take it day by day."

Grace did her best at reassurance, but something about it made me uneasy. Jake had seen us. Would he drive out to the tree farm right away?

The familiar painted Hunt's tree farm sign appeared. I shifted in my seat and attempted to look through the back window for Jake's pickup. No cars were behind us. "We need to hurry."

Noel touched my shoulder. "The police are being vigilant. Grace and I talked to them before you discharged from the hospital."

"It doesn't matter. Jake has friends everywhere, including some officers."

When we arrived in the driveway, Serenity leapt from her chair and dashed down the porch steps. Grace parked the car.

Serenity opened my passenger door. "Mommy, Mommy, Mommy, you're home."

"Hey, sweetie. We're staying at Miss Grace's house."

Noel emerged from the backseat, leaving the door open. He placed a hand on Serenity's back and directed her into the backseat. As Noel helped her buckle up, he gave a smile. "Be sure to help Miss Grace take care of your Mommy."

"We see you 'morrow?" Serenity asked.

"I have to talk with Miss Grace, but maybe Nick and I will visit you tomorrow."

"And Ford?"

Noel chucked. "And Ford."

"Thanks," I said.

Grace got out of the car and conversed with Nick and Noel for about five minutes before returning. The two men waved their goodbyes as Grace turned the car around. She fidgeted with the radio until finding a station that played Christmas tunes.

Drowsiness wiggled its way in, and my head tipped forward, only to jerk back. I couldn't fall asleep, not until we were safely at Grace's house. At the end of the driveway, a green truck hurtled past on the highway. I lurched. Jake!

"Are you okay?" Grace asked.

I gripped the armrest and focused on breathing. "Was that Jake?"

"I doubt he could drive out here that fast. Plus, Cody told me he would watch him today." Grace waited for another car to pass the driveway, and when it passed, she turned onto the highway leading to Spruce Point. She gave a glance. "When we get to my place here in a few minutes, you need to lie down and rest."

I continued checking the side mirror in case Jake had snuck behind us. He would come after us. I was sure of it.

Eighteen

Jake sneered as he pointed at the row of headstones. "It's your fault everyone died."

Upon closer examination, one headstone had Serenity's name etched into it. I screamed and crumpled against the stone. "No-o-o," I wailed.

"She's dead, just like your precious Nick." Jake guffawed, his laughter resounding.

Nick's name, along with Grace and Noel's, appeared on the other headstones. My wails transformed into shrieks. Everyone I loved had died, and it was my fault for leaving Jake. I killed them.

I had murdered them just like my parents and *him*. My voice cracked. "Why… why'd you kill them?"

"This is your punishment for forgetting that I come first!"

My daughter's form flickered until she appeared into a solid, but see-through state. She stared with glassy green eyes. "Mommy, why I dead?"

Jake's laughter increased in volume until it pierced my ears.

"Mary, wake up! You're having a nightmare." Grace's shout broke through the nightmare.

I gasped between sobs.

"Shh. You're safe here."

Light shone from the lamp and showed Grace sitting on the bed's edge. She held me as I sobbed. Though her touch caused physical pain, I needed her love for calming the mental one.

"You dreamt about Jake. Didn't you?"

I wanted to speak but couldn't.

"What your husband did to you… the abuse…" Grace straightened and caressed my hand. Her gray eyes showed softness. She whispered, "That's enough to make anyone have post-traumatic stress syndrome."

The tip of my tongue snagged over chapped, dry lips. I rubbed my lips together and smeared the spit left behind. My voice cracked. "I have to go home."

"Go home?"

I cleared my throat. "If I don't, everyone I love will die."

"You'll die, if you go back to him."

Our gaze met one another's, and a silence cloaked the bedroom. Across the hall, Serenity muttered in her sleep. Hearing her usual sleep chatter brought a small smile. Grace must have opened the bedroom door, where Serenity slept. The sheets rustled as I slid my legs over the bed's ledge opposite from where Grace sat.

"When are you going to stop punishing yourself? When Jake kills you?"

I studied the chevron pattern on the area rug.

"I know you blame yourself for most of the deaths in your life and for Nick leaving you—"

"He blames me. If I hadn't…"

"You couldn't have predicted it any more than Nick could have."

As I pushed from the bed, my teeth clamped my tongue to staunch a groan. I stood for a minute.

Grace released a sigh. "Mary, don't let the ghosts of the past turn your future into one."

"I need to check on Serenity."

"She's fine. I poked my head in there before I woke you."

The floorboards creaked in response. I needed to be sure my baby was safe. My shadow danced across the walls and floor in the nightlight's glow as I padded to Serenity's bedroom.

Serenity lay in the fetal position, babbling something about horses. She had grown fond of the Clydesdales in the two weeks I had worked at the tree farm. Tears welled, and I pressed a hand against my mouth to stifle a sob. If Serenity died, I would die this time.

"I used to do the same thing after my son was born. The thought that Carter might change his mind and kidnap our son never strayed far," Grace said in a hushed tone. "Come with me to the kitchen."

In the kitchen, water pinged against a teakettle as Grace filled it. The burner sizzled upon the teakettle's placement. Grace removed cups from a cabinet nearest the sink and dropped a tea bag in each one. "The chamomile tea should help you go back to sleep."

My arm throbbed. Yet I did not want to take a dose of a pain pill that would induce another nightmare. I slumped onto the barstool. "After your sisters helped you leave Carter, did you ever go back?"

"I did."

I stared. A woman like Grace would never go back to an abusive husband. I must have heard wrong. "What'd you say?"

"It happened a week or two after my sisters and their husbands moved me out. To be honest, I can't recall how I ended up in front of our house other than him being on my mind."

The teakettle whistled. Grace removed it from the stovetop and poured the boiling water into the cups. She set the teakettle back on a cool burner. Her voice quivered. "Carter punched me in the stomach because he was convinced the baby wasn't his."

I sniffed the wafting chamomile's flowery scent and wrapped my fingers around the steaming mug.

Her back still toward the island, Grace released a quiet sigh. She faced me but said nothing. As Grace pulled out the barstool, she finally spoke. "That was the last time I went back to him."

"Did he stalk you?"

"He did at first. I'm sure he was hoping to prove I cheated, and that the baby wasn't his. When I had my son, a nurse told me a man visited him in the nursery."

I dunked the tea bag several times and set it aside. "And he never bothered you after that?"

"No, but I always suspected he had a mistress." Grace clasped my hand and gave a tight smile. "My life got better beyond what I thought I deserved. Abusers like Jake push you down in the mud and hold you there until you suffocate. You don't want Serenity growing up thinking that's okay, do you?"

"No."

"You're not alone, and despite what you think, those deaths were out of your control. Only God has that control."

Grace had a valid point, one I struggled to accept. I did not respond. Serenity and I needed to move somewhere else where no one knew us. As long as Jake kept drinking, Spruce Point remained dangerous. He would never stop stalking us.

"Don't go thinking that running away is the best answer." Grace squeezed my hand. She swirled the tea bag inside the liquid, removed it, and took a sip. "Fear doesn't let you live either."

"If we stay, Jake will hurt anyone who helps us."

"And what happens when he finds you and Serenity alone?"

I shivered. Grace's question proved Jake would hurt us regardless until I held him accountable for that day. The cup scraped against the island. Sleepiness made its presence felt once again, and I excused myself from the kitchen.

As I passed through the living room, I paused in front of the window. A pair of unmoving headlights illuminated the street in front of Grace's house, and the streetlamp displayed a person sitting inside a dark pickup. Jake couldn't have found us that fast.

"Mary—" Grace stopped. "What's wrong?"

I whispered, "Jake found us."

"That's just my neighbor across the street. Conner usually leaves around this time for his commute to Saint Aurora."

The pickup soon disappeared down the street. Yet something within my body stated otherwise.

Nineteen

I stared at the fire until its shades of blue, orange, and red blurred. Pages rustled nearby. Grace turned the page on the book she was reading, her nails running along the edge. Distant talking surrounded me as Serenity played with her dolls. The small lump that had stuck in my throat upon waking this morning increased in size, threatening suffocation.

A soft and wet snout prodded against my hand. Ford. I stroked him, still maintaining my gaze on the fire. The aroma of coldness filled the room, sneaking past whoever had entered the house. If Ford was here, then he must have come with Nick.

Tears claimed their hold, and wetness paved a trail down my cheeks. Nick needed Ford more but allowed him to comfort me. Jake sacrificed nothing.

"Mary?" Nick's voice whispered its way into my trance.

I faced him, tears falling.

His fingers found my face, and his thumb moved along my jawline. Nick whispered. "I have a surprise for you. Will you please come with Grace and me to see what it is?"

I nodded, the lump in my throat preventing me from speaking.

"Noel's staying with Serenity."

I winced when Grace assisted with rising from the couch. My arm still ached where the doctor had performed surgery, but I hated taking the pain medication because it slowed my thinking. Jake had found us, and, if that wasn't him outside the house early this morning, he would find us soon. I needed a clear mind to escape.

"You want your medication?" Grace asked.

"No."

"At least take aspirin."

"It's nothing."

Grace held my jacket and waited as I slid my unbroken arm in the sleeve. She brought the coat around to the other side. "You're safe here. Jake doesn't know me, and the police have been patrolling the neighborhood more."

"You —small town." The words fumbled over my tongue about Jake's spies.

"If he breaks his restraining order, we report it." Grace shrugged into her own coat. "Is the stuff out there, or is it in the truck?"

"The truck," Nick replied.

"Where are we going?" I asked. It became clear Nick and Grace's surprise didn't involve the tree farm.

"Be right back, I need to warm up the car." Grace disappeared outside.

"I told you, it's a surprise." Nick shifted his body in the direction Serenity was playing. "Serenity, I have a question for you."

Serenity halted, her dolls frozen in the position she held them. She gazed at Nick. "What?"

"Will you take care of Ford until I get back?"

"Ford," Serenity squealed. She tossed the dolls aside and dashed toward the golden retriever, wrapping her arms around his throat.

Nick pulled a ball from his pocket. "This is Ford's favorite ball. I bet he'd like it if you played fetch with him."

A tingle started at my nape. Though a small gesture, it refreshed the tears of what Serenity had missed with Jake, and what he had missed by choosing liquor over his family. Would Jake consider getting help?

Grace passed the turn for the Hunt's Tree Farm and continued driving on Highway twenty-five. No one had spoken since we left her house. The car hummed, filling the quiet void between us.

I longed for home, but it had been years since I had a home. The house I shared with Jake lacked the feeling.

"We're close." Grace twisted the steering wheel to the right as she turned onto the familiar gravel road that led to my grandparents' farm. She slowed the car.

The washboard country road still jarred despite the lower speed Grace drove. She apologized for its roughness.

A single mile seemed like hundreds by the time we crossed the metal bridge. Several feet from the stream, an old truck lay mangled in a grove of dead trees because of the 1927 flood. As we entered the driveway, my grandparents' two-story house provided a balm to my aching heart.

Like Serenity and I had seen the last time, a construction dumpster remained in the yard. No other vehicles were parked in the driveway. "It's Sunday. Construction workers don't work on Sunday," I muttered.

Grace parked the car. "We're here."

"I don't understand. Why are we here?" I fumbled with the door handle.

"Remember when your grandparents were in trouble?" Nick said. "I bought them out."

A quiet gasp escaped. All this time, I thought the owner had abandoned my grandparents' former home.

"I had bought it with the pipedream of following in your grandparents' footsteps." Nick never elaborated beyond that statement. Perhaps he didn't for my sake.

"You didn't bring me out here to show me your house."

"You're right," Grace said. She got out of the car and opened the trunk.

"When's the last time you went shooting?" Nick asked.

I shrugged.

"You haven't practiced since I left?"

"What's your point? Why are we shooting today?"

The trunk slammed shut. Grace strolled past my window, carrying a black case and a target of some sort. She gestured, which meant get out of the car and assist Nick in following her.

"I'm gonna teach you how to shoot one-handed. It's just in case you need to defend yourself against Jake."

"Get out of the car. Grace wants us to follow her."

Nick's door swung open, and he stood. "You're lucky Jake didn't kill you… this time."

"I won't kill Jake."

"You might say that. But when it comes to your life versus his life, you will."

"You two coming?" Grace reappeared, hands on her hips. She dropped them to her side and walked toward Nick. "You can use my arm."

Nick took her arm, and they glided ahead while I lagged behind.

I smiled at Serenity's being aghast at the toilet being thrown from our last visit. Grandma Hazel should have shared more of her childhood stories, or had I failed at remembering them? At Serenity's age, she probably would have been appalled at the toilet thing too.

In the backyard, Grace stopped with Nick near the black case and target. "We're here. How far do you want the target?"

"Let's start at twenty-five feet."

"The gun case is by your right foot. I'll go set up the target while you walk Mary through the steps."

Nick squatted and groped for the case, unsnapping it and removing what I assumed was a nine-millimeter. He removed the magazine. "Mary, you ready?"

"No. Because you're talking about killing my husband."

"Look, I never thought I'd kill anyone either until being deployed." Nick rose and left the magazine inside the open case. "It wasn't until that first time insurgents attacked my unit. Then I understood to kill or be killed."

"What about the IED explosion?"

Nick's jaw clenched for a brief second, and then slackened. "Shooting one-handed is different from two-handed. You were an excellent shot, so humor me with this one-handed thing."

"You're not giving me a choice, are you?" I sighed.

"Nope. If you won't do it for yourself, then do it for Serenity. That little girl will remember what Jake did to you for the rest of her life, and how she thought you were dead."

I winced at how he had stabbed me in the heart with those words. Nick was right. My parents' demise still haunted me fifteen years later. Remembering the car accident during the blizzard stopped me that night from getting Jake at Orson's.

"What do I need to know for shooting one-handed?"

"I'll demonstrate. Can you please turn me so the gun isn't pointed at Grace?"

"Turn to your left."

Nick complied but continued pointing the gun at the ground. "Am I clear to show you? I'm taking precautions just in case the gun does fire."

"Yeah."

"Position your feet first." Nick placed his left foot behind the other and bent his right knee forward. He raised his shooting arm. "Make sure you keep your elbow loose, but not too loose. Then lock your wrist."

"What happens if I don't?"

"If you don't, your wrist will jerk around while you're shooting. By keeping your wrist straight, you're more likely to hit the target. Just make sure you don't grip the gun too tight though."

Nick resumed his shooting stance. "See how I'm holding the gun? I'm holding it straight because my wrist and forearm are straight."

I examined how he held the gun. It dredged up memories of when we went shooting. If my arm hadn't been broken, remembering how to shoot would be easier than learning this one-handed technique.

Grace strolled toward us. "You get it figured out, Mary?"

Nick loosened his shooting position and [pointed the gun's barrel at the ground. "Before we load it, I want Mary to copy what I showed her."

"Grace, do you know how to shoot one-handed?" I asked.

"I learned from my women's empowerment classes. When you're all healed, you should take them."

"Maybe." My hand clasped over Nick's, and he transferred the gun's grip. I reenacted what Nick had shown. The gun held solely in my right hand felt unsteady and wrong. "Is this right?"

"I… I…" Nick stammered.

"You have my permission to *see*." I closed my eyes and waited. If he could have seen me in the hospital, Jake would have been dead. As long as Nick didn't touch my face, the ugliness of what Jake had done remained hidden.

Twenty

My daughter crossed her arms over her chest, and scrunched her lips together. Serenity glared and dropped her narrowed eyes toward the floor, muttering a whine. "But I wanna see the horsies!"

"We can't go to the tree farm today."

"Why-y-y?"

"Because Daddy might find us there."

Serenity loosened her arms and lifted her gaze from the floor. She remained quiet.

No three-year-old should have understood what we were going through. Yet Serenity wanted what any child wanted. I swallowed. She deserved time outside without worrying about her daddy coming to hurt us. To be honest, I felt stir-crazy too.

Dishes clinked against the table. The aroma of chicken broth lingered in the living room. "Lunch is ready," Grace called out.

Serenity broke eye contact and ambled into the kitchen, where Grace asked her to wash her hands. A chair shrieked across the floor.

While they conversed with one another, I opened Grace's flip phone and strolled through her contacts, stopping at Noel's name. I glanced toward the kitchen. "'Fear doesn't let you live either,'" I murmured what Grace had said during our conversation about Jake the other morning.

Each unanswered ring stripped away more of my hope. By the eleventh ring, I prepared to hang up when Nick answered. "Hello?"

The phone slipped from my ear. I caught the flip phone and stared at it.

"Hello? *Hello?*"

"Nick? Why are you answering Noel's phone?"

"Mary?"

"Where's—" The doorbell startled me, and I gasped. As I peeked through the window, Noel waited in front of the door. "Never mind, Noel's here."

I ended the call before Nick could respond.

Grace had rounded the corner by the time I unlocked the door and let Noel in. She smiled. "You made it."

Noel returned the smile. He removed his red coat and draped it over the back of the chair, leaving on his Santa hat.

"Santa's here." A giggle came from behind Grace. Serenity leaned just enough to peek then jerked upright to hide herself. "You bwing the horsies?"

"Sorry, I forgot them at the tree farm. Do you think they would have eaten knoephla soup and egg salad sandwiches with us?"

Serenity chortled. "No-o-o."

Though I couldn't see her, she would have scrunched her face during that reply. That look was one I had become familiar with since her birth. When Grace and Noel exchanged glances, I made my departure for the kitchen and stopped where Serenity stood. I brushed along her sleeve. "Come on. Let's go eat."

Serenity obeyed without a whine.

Before entering the kitchen, I took a last glance at Grace and Noel. I assumed they were discussing us. Five minutes later, they joined us at the island.

"You and Serenity should get out of here for the afternoon," Grace said as she ladled the knoephla soup into her bowl. "The fresh air will cure your restlessness."

"What about…?"

Noel set his sandwich on the plate. "Even if he shows, I doubt anything would happen. Perhaps we could go for a sleigh ride or a walk through the trees."

"Can Ford come?" Serenity asked while chewing.

"Please don't talk with your mouth full," I scolded my daughter. "Remember? Ford isn't a pet."

"Cuz he helps Nick?"

"That's right, honey."

"What wrong with Nick?"

Tightness began in my chest at her innocent question. I recalled the day at the grocery store with Nick and Ford. In Serenity's purview, Ford was just a dog. She understood Ford belonged to Nick but didn't quite understand he worked for him. Her understanding was still better than the children that stared at Nick and Ford.

"You'll have to ask him," Noel said.

"Mommy say no go to tree farm."

I did not speak but savored the creamy soup with its flavors of rich chicken broth. Grace had made the simple soup hearty by adding extra carrots, knoephla, and potatoes. The knoephla soup tasted similar to Grandma Hazel's recipe. I swallowed.

Silence had fallen at the table, and everyone stared at me.

"Fine… we can go to the tree farm."

Serenity squealed. Her spoon flipped out of the bowl and clattered against the table.

My stomach churned at the decision. Jake would find out we were there. The question remained if his spies saw us, and how fast they would contact Jake.

In the man-made forest, birds and squirrels chattered amongst the distant noise of chainsaws and machinery. Nick and I ambled on the trail, the snow crunching underneath our boots. Neither of us spoke. As we trudged along, I continually scanned through the trees and the trail ahead for anyone that might be spying.

"You don't seem very relaxed," Nick said.

"I'm worried about Serenity." The lie slipped off my tongue without trying. Serenity was safe with Noel. Far too long I had lied to keep others from discovering my secrets.

Nick scoffed. "I doubt that."

"Sorry."

"Don't be. It's me you're talking to."

"Do you remember that day Jake was here, and I said he needed to talk to me?"

Nick nodded.

"Jake told me his friend, Ollie, mentioned I worked here. I thought Ollie worked at the lumber mill?"

"That— what…" Nick muttered the rest of his sentence. He halted, the harness jerking against Ford. His jaw clenched. "Ollie will be dealt with."

I gaped. A man emerged through the trees and stopped like he was watching us.

"Mary?"

"I think Noel should take us back to Grace's."

"What? Why? You two haven't been here long."

"Nick," I whispered, "he's watching us."

"Ollie!"

The man sprinted and disappeared farther into the forest.

Nick removed a cellphone from his coat pocket and prompted it to call Noel. The phone replied with a 'calling Noel.'

My heartbeat kicked to a faster speed. Jake was on his way. I tugged on Nick's arm. "We need to go."

"Noel's not answering." Nick jammed the cellphone back into his pocket.

"Ollie called him. I know it."

"Look. If he did, that doesn't mean Jake will do anything except beg you to come home."

"You can't predict that. Jake's not the same person he was when you two were friends." I shook my head and let out a huff. "This is your fault. You abandoned him like you left me."

"I'm sorry, but you're wrong. Anyway, forget it." Nick turned Ford around and directed him to find home. His pace increased.

I struggled to keep up with Nick's new pace and soon fell behind. My arm ached. When the pain intensified, I slowed to a stop. Perhaps I should have stayed and rested at Grace's.

"Mary? Are you okay?"

"No, my arm hurts. Going for a walk like this was a bad idea."

Nick stopped. "I'm not sure what Jake told you about our falling out. He had a drinking problem back then too."

I closed my eyes. Jake had been drinking far longer than I had known, and he probably drank throughout our dating. How could I have missed the signs before we got married?

"I've heard about Jake sobering up and then falling back into his drinking again."

"Was he the one who broke your nose and gave you the shiner?" I remembered the day Nick had come home a mess. Although he never said what happened, I had suspected something happened between him and Jake for them to part ways.

Nick swiveled his head to the left. "I think you know the answer to that."

"Why didn't you tell me?"

"We had other things to worry about at the time, like our move to Saint Aurora."

I took a step and sucked in a burning breath. Nick had lost the real Jake to alcohol the same way I did. "You should have helped him."

"Don't you think I tried? No one can help Jake unless he helps himself first." Nick paused. "We're almost to the house. Let's get you aspirin before the pain gets too bad."

'No one can help Jake unless he helps himself first' reiterated itself on the remaining walk to the house. The statement held a truth. I could plead Jake to do rehab, but none of it would stick unless he confronted his demons. His preference seemed to be drowning them.

Whenever I asked Jake about his childhood, he refused to talk about it. "Nick, do you know what Jake's childhood was like?"

Nick held open the door. "Not much to tell, but I'll tell you once you've taken something for your arm."

Twenty-One

I paced in front of the window and around Grace's living room. Despite yesterday's run-in with Ollie in the forest, Jake never showed at the tree farm. His pickup never followed us either after we left Nick's. Uneasiness still clung.

A green truck rumbled to a stop across the street. The butterflies in my stomach turned into a bucking horse as I waited for what would happen next. The driver slammed the door. When they faced the window, I gasped.

Connor waved and walked down the sidewalk toward his house.

I should have relaxed, but the tension wound itself tighter, like a stubborn burr. This time it was Grace's neighbor. The days blurred together since my release from the hospital. Jake should have found us already. Was Connor across the street a spy for Jake? Perhaps that's why Jake never approached us because someone was reporting to him.

"Mary," Grace said.

I turned away from the window and discovered Grace staring.

"The temperature is supposed to be near thirty today. I think we should drive to your grandparents' old place and practice shooting again."

"What about Serenity?"

"She can come with."

I shook my head. "I don't want her around guns."

"Nick said the house is almost finished. I know he and Noel were going out there today to clean the barn before the construction crew starts on that in the New Year. Between the barn and house, Noel and I can keep Serenity busy."

"Grace? What's the date today?"

"The twenty-third. Why?"

I tucked a bothersome strand of hair behind my ear and murmured, "Serenity's presents."

In my haze, I had forgotten about the upcoming holidays. What kind of mother was I? Between Grace, Nick, and Noel's help, I couldn't ask them for anymore. A light touch on my shoulder startled me.

Grace whispered, "Don't worry. If you believe in Christmas magic, you won't be disappointed."

I chuckled. Her statement seemed like something Noel would say. With Serenity convinced Noel was Santa, I suspected Grace was Mrs. Claus.

"Okay. Call Noel to let him know we'll come."

"Serenity's in her room playing. I'll call Noel and make a lunch basket to bring with." Grace gestured at the kitchen. "I forgot my phone on the island."

After Grace departed, I stared through the window again. Another green pickup idled past. I shuddered despite not getting a clear glimpse of the driver. All green trucks looked the same as Jake's. Distant talking from the kitchen forced me to leave my post for Serenity's room.

Serenity's voice carried into the hallway. "Dear Santa…"

I paused near her room and stole a peek inside.

My daughter sat in the center of the room with a paper on the floor and a crayon in her hand. Serenity squinted, and the tip of her tongue stuck out like she was deep in thought. She scribbled across the paper. "For Chwistmas I want a Daddy that doesn't hurt my mommy and me."

A swallow remained stuck in my throat. In punishing myself, I had punished her, too, in my self-imposed hell with Jake. I continued standing in the doorway.

My nearly four-year-old babbled and scrawled more, then signed her name at the bottom. She deserved to attend a preschool.

Grace shuffled along the hallway and stopped behind me. "Is she writing a letter to Santa?"

"I'm a terrible mother. She asked Santa for a daddy who doesn't hurt us."

"No, you're not. You protected her when Jake went after her."

"Did you know Jake wouldn't let me sign her up for preschool? Serenity's never played with other kids. What if I sign her up, and she fails or doesn't make friends at preschool?"

Our eyes met. "Serenity's smart, and so are you. Even smart people make mistakes."

"Mommy? Can we give this to Santa?" Serenity asked.

"Sure, honey." My gaze traveled to Serenity, and I smiled at the way she clutched at the letter for Santa. Noel wouldn't be able to read it. "Noel's going to be at Nick's new house. You could give it to him."

"How about we bring Nick and Noel on a picnic?" Grace asked.

"And Ford too?"

I nodded. "And Ford too."

Gravel pinged and clunked underneath the car, slowing as Grace turned into the driveway that led to my grandparents' place. A loud rumble sped past. The passenger side mirror displayed a dot of green zooming farther down the road. Jake had followed us. I had seen too many green pickups today for it to be a coincidence.

Noel and Nick waited on the porch while Ford lay by Nick's feet. When Grace parked the car, the two men rose.

I opened the car door with a grunt.

"Wait. Let me help you," Grace said, rushing from her seat. By the time she reached the passenger side, I had gotten out of the car.

"I'm fine." I stumbled, and Grace jerked to catch me. "Really."

I pushed by Grace and ambled a few steps before stopping. My gaze traveled along the country road in search of the green truck. A nose nudged the back of my leg.

"Mary?" Nick asked. "Something's bothering you. What is it?"

"Do you remember Cotton?"

"Your horse? Yeah, I remember."

"I feel like her, trapped."

Nick lowered his voice. "I feel trapped too."

We stood in silence. I stared at the barn and the empty corral with its rotted boards. Cotton paced around, waiting to be freed. She had been sold along with the rest of my grandparents' horses after Grandpa died. I sniffled at the memory of saying goodbye to my loyal friend.

Serenity's giggle mingled with Grace and Noel's banter.

"Let's go for a walk," Nick said.

"Where?"

"Doesn't matter. Sometimes it's nice not having a destination in mind."

We shuffled alongside each other in the driveway without speaking. When the others grew distant, Nick cleared his throat. "After I lost my sight, I wished the IED explosion would have killed me too. It was like all the darkness had locked me inside a cage that I couldn't escape."

Nick hesitated. "Some days my restlessness threatens to boil over, and I get frustrated at not being able to do things like I used to."

I clasped Nick's hand, and he stifled a small gasp. We both stopped. If Nick could see, our gazes would have danced with one another like they did long ago. I sighed. "I trapped myself by not leaving Jake sooner when he first started hurting me."

"And you still feel that way?"

"He's stalking us. I can't help but think if I would have left sooner that he wouldn't be doing this."

"Jake still wouldn't have let you go so easily." Nick's lips contorted like he wanted to say more. He didn't.

Our regrets remained unspoken. The roar of an engine reverberated in the distance. I began to release Nick's hand, but he clung to it. "Nick."

"I don't blame you for what happened."

"What?"

"Not waiting for me. For…" Nick murmured, "for… his death."

"His crib is in the barn. I didn't know Grandpa and Grandma saved it until two or three weeks ago when Serenity snuck into the barn."

"You and Serenity were in the barn?"

Tires skidded at the end of the driveway. We both glanced. A green pickup slid to a halt, and the driver's door bounced back as someone got out.

"Who's here?"

I shoved Nick's hand away and dropped mine at my side. "Jake," I croaked.

Jake approached closer.

"Mary, why don't you go into the house? I'll talk to Jake."

Ford growled and inched forward but found himself unable to go any farther.

"Easy, boy," Nick said to Ford.

"I'm not leaving you alone with him."

Jake stomped toward us, splattering mud and ice from the road. "Well, well, well. What do you think you're doing with *my* wife?"

"We're just talkin'."

"You can't be here," I pleaded.

"Drop the charges and come home so we can work this out."

Nick clenched his jaw. "I'm sorry, Jake. But I won't let her or Serenity go home with you. You need help first before you work things out with your wife."

"I bet that hurt for you to say, *your wife*," Jake jeered.

Nick winced. A fist bunched at his side but did not move. "You're trespassing on private property. I suggest you leave before I call the police."

Jake sniggered. He tossed his arms out to the sides and held them there with a sneer. "You too scared to fight me now that you're blind?"

"Just because my eyes don't work, doesn't mean my fists—"

"Stop it! You go through rehab and counseling first, and then we'll talk."

"Fine. I'll go to an AA meeting tonight if that's what you want. Will you come home tomorrow?" Jake asked.

"I'll think about it." I waited for Nick to protest, but he never did.

Jake lowered his arms and glared. "If you don't, I'll find you."

I clamped my tongue between my teeth and forced a nod. The lie I had given Jake would pacify him, or at least until tomorrow when he realized we weren't coming home to celebrate Christmas. As if on autopilot, my lips feigned a smile.

"I'll show you tomorrow that I can change," Jake muttered before marching back to his truck.

The driver's door slammed. Gravel flew behind as the pickup revved down the road. Only when the engine's hum couldn't be heard did I allow myself to breathe. My chest burned. Jake would return to Grace's house and spy on us.

"You okay?" Nick asked.

"We should practice shooting in case Jake does that again."

Twenty-Two

Christmas Eve

In the church parking lot, I searched for any signs that Jake had followed. A green pickup whizzed past. Jake. My mouth dried, and I swallowed, but ended with a coughing fit. He followed us to church.

"Here, take a drink of water." Grace offered a water bottle and glanced in the direction I had been looking.

The water did little at calming my insides. We should have stayed at her house instead of going to the Christmas Eve church service. I dropped the water bottle upon a tug on my coat. "Damn it," I muttered.

"Mommy."

"It's okay. If you need more water, the church has water bottles in the kitchen." Grace bent over and picked up the half-empty water bottle, pouring the rest out. She replaced the cap on it. "We should go inside. The service starts soon."

Serenity clasped her hand in mine. "Mommy? We sing tonight?"

I stared at the brick building and its stained-glass windows that depicted the story of Jesus' crucifixion. A simple manger display decorated the front of the church. Though I had attended this church before, it now seemed like a stranger.

People passed by in the parking lot, exclaiming 'Merry Christmas' with a smile. I couldn't remember the last time Jake stayed home on a Christmas Eve. Organ music seeped outside each time people entered the church. Someone gave a nudge.

"Mommy."

Grace replied, "Can you hear the music? We'll be singing lots of Christmas songs tonight to celebrate Jesus' birth."

"Come on, Mommy. Let's go sing." Serenity led me toward the church just as a green pickup idled along on the street.

I whispered a silent prayer that it wasn't Jake.

We crossed the foyer and into the worship center, seating ourselves on a pew in the center. The organ finished its last note. Grace pulled a hymnal and flipped the page to the listed song on the board. As the organist began the opening song, Grace whispered to Serenity, "We're going to sing a song about angels. I'll help you sing it if you don't know the words."

Grace's soprano voice mingled with the others in singing "Angels We Have Heard on High."

I shifted back and forth, unable to get comfortable. Tonight's church celebration did little to keep me from perusing the crowd for Jake's face. People smiled as they caught my gaze. A lump developed in my throat at the memories this church had held in my youth and young adult life. Seeing all the families at tonight's celebration provided a reminder of what I had lost in the last decade. I stared at the farthest pew on the opposite side of the room and gave a quiet gasp. Jake *was* here.

His icy eyes glared back, unmoving. It took us leaving for him to come inside the church.

I avoided his glare and brought my focus to the altar, stepping closer to Grace. "He's here," I murmured.

Grace stopped singing. "Where?"

"Four pews down to our right."

Grace slowly glanced over her shoulder. "I don't see him."

"What? He was just there."

His seat was empty. Had I imagined him sitting there? I scanned each pew but no sign of Jake. A figure moved about near the back. I clamped the side of my tongue between my teeth as the person stopped.

Jake gave a smirk. He pointed at me then himself and mouthed words along the lines of 'you belong to me.'

I gaped as he turned and disappeared through the doorway into the foyer. My muscles tensed. He'd be waiting to follow us when church was finished. This was the first Christmas Eve Jake spent alone, not that he celebrated much with us. A hand on my arm startled me.

"What's wrong?" Grace asked.

"Jake threatened me."

"Is he still here?"

"I don't know. He went into the foyer, but I can't see if he left the building."

"After the service, we'll find Cody and ask if he can escort us home."

"Please be seated," the pastor said.

Everyone in the church shuffled into a sitting position. The pastor started the story of Mary and Joseph traveling to the inn.

I stared at the statue of Mary until she became a haze through my tear-filled eyes. We should have never stayed here. The pastor's sermon faded out. Serenity and I should have left Spruce Point. No… it wouldn't have mattered because Jake still would have found us.

Noel and Nick met us in the foyer. Some worshippers left while others meandered downstairs for fellowship. As people passed by, most stared at Nick and Ford the same way they did that day at the grocery store. An occasional person would stop and give Nick a 'welcome home.'

When the foyer cleared out, Noel kneeled in front of Serenity. He winked. "We better go downstairs because I heard Santa might hand out presents."

"Noel…" I stammered. How does one approach the subject of stalking in front of your daughter? "I uh…"

"Is everything all right? Your hand is shaking." Noel rose, cocking his head.

"He…"

Noel nodded as he understood my babble. "As long as we're in a crowd, I doubt he would do anything except watch. If you're that uneasy, we'll stay long enough for Serenity to see Santa. Is that okay?"

"Please, Mommy," Serenity begged.

After seeing her pleading green eyes, I shoved down my anxiousness that something was going to happen.

I ruffled Serenity's hair and hugged her. "Once you see Santa, we're leaving."

Noel pushed back his shirt sleeve and revealed a wristwatch. "Santa should come in about a half hour, or so I've been told."

"Fine," I replied.

Serenity dashed to the top of the steps and halted, spinning around. Although Serenity didn't say anything, her foot tapped while she waited for the rest of us. When we neared, she skipped down the steps.

"Remember what I said about jumping on the steps?" Nick asked.

A heavy sigh came from Serenity, and her shoulders drooped. "No jumpin' on the stairs." She continued downward to the church basement without jumping.

"When you get to the bottom, you can jump," Nick teased.

Serenity hastened her step. True to her character, she jumped from the bottom of the staircase and whirled around.

"Serenity, you wait for us," I chastised. Until we returned to Grace's house, I wasn't letting her stray far.

Chatter, singing, and piano music filled the fellowship hall. The church ladies worked behind the kitchen counter, arranging platters of bars, cookies, and Christmas candy. An orange, tangy aroma wafted. I tipped my nose upwards and sniffed. "What is that? It smells delicious."

"That's Nell's famous wassail." Grace grinned. "She makes it every year for the Christmas Eve gathering, and it's to die for."

"I'll finagle us some. Serenity, you can come with me and help pick out what to eat, if it's okay with your mommy." Noel raised an eyebrow.

"Only if you bring back a cornflake wreath for me," I jested.

As Noel and Serenity walked toward the counter and beverage table, I examined the room for anyway that Jake might sneak into the crowd. Like Noel had said earlier, the only thing Jake could do was watch. The fire doors were locked on the outside. Jake would have to come through the only door in the fellowship hall.

"He's not here, Mary," Grace said.

"You don't know Jake."

"Noel and I will watch for you." Grace took my hand and gave it a squeeze. "Right now, let's find a table so you can try to relax."

Grace, Nick, and I slumped at a table with a sightline of the entrance. Ford tucked himself underneath the table and on my feet.

Noel carried a tray of drinks while Serenity ran ahead with a plate filled with goodies. She slammed the plate onto the table. "Mommy, guess what?"

"What?"

"I got hot chocolate!"

A burst of laughter rumbled from Nick's chest. "She's a chocaholic just like Grandma Hazel I see."

I had forgotten about Grandma Hazel's chocolate obsession. The small things in remembering her were fading, and I hated it. "Oh, I think Serenity might be worse. If she had it her way, she wouldn't drink anything else."

After a half hour, Santa arrived like Noel had promised. Noel stood in line with Serenity and had promised to take a picture of her sitting on Santa's lap.

Though I started to relax, I continued doing a room sweep. My eyes stopped on a man standing alone in a dim corner. I squinted and tried to determine if it was Jake. When he reappeared out of the corner, a silent sigh escaped. It wasn't Jake.

I glanced at Santa and found Serenity sitting on his lap. Noel stood in front of him, snapping a photo of them smiling. After he took their photo, Serenity talked with Santa for a minute, and when she finished, Santa gave her a small, wrapped box.

Serenity rushed to our table. "Santa gave me a present."

Without waiting for a prompt from me, she tore the wrapping paper off and revealed a chocolate orange. She held it up with a grin. "Chocolate!"

"You have to wait until tomorrow," I said and took the box from her.

"Can I go play?"

"Only a few more minutes, then we're leaving."

As my daughter skipped away, I longed for her unawareness. Sleep beckoned my name, yet I couldn't because of Jake haunting me both physically and in my dreams. I turned my gaze from her.

"You coming tomorrow to the tree farm for Christmas?" Nick asked.

"It depends on Jake." I swiveled my head and looked for my daughter. My insides somersaulted with each passing second I didn't find her. "Serenity?"

"She's with the Michelson twins," Grace said. She and Noel exchanged glances with one another. Without her saying a word, Noel left the table to fetch Serenity.

Twenty-Three

Glass shattered from below. Jake. I bolted upright in bed and blinked at the glowing alarm clock. It was after midnight. Boots thudded in a random pattern, as if stumbling. I fumbled for my hidden gun in the nightstand and cringed as it scraped against the drawer.

Jake muttered something, his voice carrying. Another crash sounded.

Grace met me in the hallway, carrying her own weapon. She whispered, "The phone is beside my bed. Call the police. I'm gonna confront him."

"Where's my wife?" Jake shouted.

"No, he's looking for me. You take care of Serenity," I replied in a hushed tone and gripped the gun. Nick had trained me for this moment, not to kill, but for protection. My stomach churned. If it came down to it, could I shoot Jake?

"Mary," Jake slurred, raising his voice. "I want you and Serenity home."

The door to Serenity's bedroom opened. She emerged through the doorway and rubbed her eyes while mumbling. "Is that Daddy?"

"Let's go into your room, honey." Grace guided Serenity into her bedroom and murmured, "I don't like this."

I tiptoed to the top of the steps and peered into the living room. A chill prickled the hairs on my neck. Between the moonlight and streetlamp, Jake's form leaned against the couch's armrest.

Jake hollered my name again. He rose sharply and tripped, most likely on the area rug. A string of cuss words flowed from his mouth as if it were a single word. He scrambled upward by using the couch armrest.

I forced myself to say his name.

"Go get Serenity and get your asses down here. You're coming home."

"No."

Jake moved forward, stomping the floor. "You listen to me. You're my wife, and I said you're coming home!"

"Go home, Jake, and get help." I walked down three steps and pressed the gun against my leg, prepared to reveal it if needed. "You need to talk to someone about your drinking and hurting us."

"If you'd listen to me, I wouldn't have to," Jake retorted as he neared the bottom of the staircase.

"You're violating your restraining order. I've called the police, so I suggest you go home before they get here," Grace said.

"You! It's your fault my girls left me." Jake gripped the railing and lifted his foot.

I hid the gun behind my back and took another step. Goosebumps raced up and down my body, and my insides trembled as the gap between Jake and I grew closer. "Wait. We can talk in the living room. Serenity's sleeping, and we don't want to wake her."

Jake said nothing. Though I couldn't be sure, his fists clenched and unclenched.

"Please?" I pleaded, stopping in front of him. This was a mistake getting this close to him. I knew what would be next but had to do this. Serenity didn't need to see what was unfolding, for she had already seen too much in her young life.

Jake raised a hand, and I fought to keep from flinching when he caressed my cheek. "I love you," he whispered, "please come home."

I shook my head. "Not yet. Not until you get help."

"You're my wife." Jake clamped my jaw. "You don't get to say no to me."

"You're hurting me." The gun dropped on the step with a thud. I tried to pry his fingers off my jaw, but it was futile.

"Let her go right now," Grace demanded.

"Or what?"

"The police are on their way."

I yelped as Jake tightened his grip on my jaw and gave a tug, causing me to stagger downward on the last step.

"I said 'let her go.'"

Jake didn't listen and whirled around with me continuing to teeter. He marched toward the door, dragging me along.

The living room lights flicked on, and Grace called out. "Stop or I'll shoot."

Jake halted. Without saying a word, he released me with a laugh.

When I walked away, he shoved me against the sideboard and wall. Pictures and figurines crashed onto the floor.

"Mary! Are you okay?" Grace asked.

Jake charged toward her, his boots thudding against the floor. Before she could fire, Jake tackled her. The gun careened across the floor while they fought, each fighting for control. Jake punched Grace, and she yelped.

As they wrestled each other, I remained frozen as if a spectator. Grace crossed her arms above her face while Jake pummeled her with no hint of stopping. "Mary belongs with me," he snarled.

"Mary, get the gun," Grace shouted, her words stretched out in slow-motion.

Though I heard her plea, I did not act on it.

"Mommy!" Serenity's shrill voice pierced through my stupor. She stood near the top of the stairway, staring at Jake and Grace.

I dashed toward the gun.

"Daddy!"

The lone word reverberated, overlapping with Serenity's shrieks of 'stop it.' I fumbled with the gun as it continued to slide on the floor. When I got a firm hold on the gun, I swiveled the barrel toward Jake. "I have the gun, Jake."

Jake paused with his beating. He twisted toward me with a sneer and a huff. "You won't shoot me. I'm your husband."

Nick's teachings whispered in my ear. I assumed the position of putting weight on my right leg and outstretched the gun. Jake and I stared at each other, neither breaking eye contact.

"And who taught you that? Nick?" Jake jeered.

I gave the gun a wave. "Go home! I'm tired of you hurting us."

Jake gaped. He got off Grace and whirled around, kicking her in the ribs. "You brainwashed my wife."

He lifted his foot to kick again.

"Please don't make me shoot you," I begged.

His foot dropped back on the floor. Jake faced me and scoffed, "Shoot me then."

He extended his arms to the side and stepped forward. "We both know you're coming home with me, and you're gonna be a good wife like I want you to be."

Serenity appeared above Grace, and I gasped. My gun! Our daughter placed her hands on her hips. "You mean, Daddy. Get outta here."

"You're coming home with me and Mommy," Jake replied, his eyes narrowing. "Just as soon as Mommy puts the gun down."

I inched forward. "Serenity, go upstairs."

"No." Serenity bent down and retrieving my gun. "I gots my own gun too."

Oh, God.

"Give me the gun." Jake held out his hand.

"No!"

Jake stormed toward her, and I squeezed the trigger. The gunfire mingled with screams, though I couldn't tell whose they were. I rushed to Serenity as Jake toppled. Red and blue lights swirled in front of the window.

I clutched Serenity and discovered she still held my gun while I had dropped Grace's along the way. "Drop the gun on the stair, sweetie."

Shouting ensued, followed by police entering Grace's house. I wrapped an arm around Serenity tighter as someone yelled for an ambulance. A sob burst. I slumped on the step and leaned against the wall with Serenity. Her face buried beneath my arm. Oh, God, what had I done?

Twenty-Four

I shot Jake. The bloodstain on Grace's floor became a dark blur from where my husband had lain. 'When it comes to, it's your life versus his life, you will,' I repeated Nick's words he had said the day we went shooting. I swayed with Serenity.

"Miss?" a woman officer kneeled in front of us. "Is there anyone we can call to pick up your daughter?"

I kept rocking.

"Call Noel," Grace croaked. She winced as a paramedic examined her. "He's at Hunt's Tree Farm."

"I'd heard Nick Hunt was back." The woman stood and retrieved her cellphone. She strolled around the corner and into the kitchen, speaking to whoever answered.

I shot Jake.

"Mommy, you're squeezing me too hard."

I murmured, "Sorry."

"Is…" Serenity glanced up with a red streaked face, her green eyes still containing tears. "… Daddy going to die?"

Oh, God! I shot him in front of my daughter. How had I let it come to this? We should have left him sooner and fled town. We… we should have gone home with him. I fought to suck in air, my chest growing tighter with each passing second. I shot my husband!

"Miss." Someone shook me. It sounded like the woman officer. "Breathe. You gotta breathe."

I couldn't. The ugly scenario replayed in a loop, and blood splatter flew from Jake's back. I. Shot. A. Person. What's wrong with me? My husband was at the hospital because I shot him. I shivered. If he died, I would be a murderer.

Serenity would always remember Christmas Eve as being tainted because her mommy shot her daddy. Oh, God, I scarred her for life.

"Miss," the woman officer exclaimed.

Through my tear-blurred vision, I learned she was the same officer who had notified me in the hospital about Jake being jailed. "Is… is… is he going to survive?" I asked, barely inaudible.

"The last I heard, he was rushed into surgery."

"Oh, God," I wailed. My throat burned from the onslaught of wracking sobs.

"Judging by what happened, it seems like self-defense." The woman officer squatted in front of Serenity and me. Her voice softened. "He wouldn't have stopped. Let's move into the kitchen away from the blood."

The woman officer helped me up, and like a mother leading a child, she ushered both Serenity and I into the kitchen. She perused the cupboards until finding glasses and brought us water. "There. Nick and Noel should be here soon."

"And Ford," Serenity said.

Serenity's need to include Ford brought a small smile. "Thanks… I didn't catch your name," I muttered.

"You can call me Katie."

I sipped on the water, its coolness soothing the burning in my throat. After Nick and Noel came, I needed to get to the hospital. Jake was still my husband. The radio chattered on Katie's jacket, and I strained to understand the jargon.

Katie gave a closed smile.

"Mommy? Will Santa still bwing me presents?

"Oh, Honey, of course he will." I swallowed. Would the police let us take her Christmas presents? Grace's house was a crime scene.

Grace hobbled into the kitchen, followed by Nick and Noel.

"Where's Ford?" Serenity bobbed her head while searching for her furry companion.

Nick teased, "I think you like Ford more than you like me."

Serenity whimpered and then started crying.

"Ford's waiting for you in the car. You're gonna go to the tree farm with Grace and Noel, that is, if the police are done with her?"

"Cody got my statement and said he'd call if there were any more questions," Grace replied. "I should go to the hospital with Mary. Someone should be with her."

"I'm going with her," Nick responded.

I nudged Noel. "Serenity's suitcase is upstairs, the second bedroom on the left. Could you please get it?"

"Grace, let me help you upstairs. You're staying at the tree farm too, so pack a bag." Noel offered an elbow to Grace.

When their footsteps distanced themselves from the kitchen, I took Nick's hand and whispered, "You should go with them."

"No, you need someone with you who's been through what you have." Nick matched my hushed tone. He didn't elaborate, and I suspected he did it for Serenity's sake.

I glanced at my daughter and found she had dozed off. My own eyes demanded sleep. What time was it? I searched for a clock, discovering it was past one. It was Christmas morning.

"Mary?" Katie asked.

I jerked. She had been quiet, so quiet that I forgot for a moment Katie existed.

"I'm sorry, didn't mean to scare you. I was going to say it would be okay to bring…" Katie gestured at Serenity and mouthed 'presents.' The radio chatter began again, and she silenced it. "Excuse me. I have to take this."

My stomach wrenched. Were they radioing her that Jake died? Had I become a murderer?

Each time a doctor or nurse passed by the waiting room, I forced myself to keep sitting instead of leaping from my chair. An hour passed since Katie had brought Nick and me to the hospital. The atmosphere between the three of us was silence. I wanted news on Jake, good or bad.

Katie kept studying me.

I sighed. "You haven't interviewed me yet, so let's hear it."

"Tell me what happened."

"Jake broke into Grace's house. I confronted him, and he hit me then attacked Grace when she intervened."

"And?" Katie asked.

"I managed to get Grace's gun, which had slid across the floor during their fight. But I couldn't do it. After that, my daughter came downstairs."

"Is that when she found your gun on the step?"

I glanced at Nick, who remained unmoving in his slumped position. Was he listening, or had he fallen asleep? Sunglasses hid his blue eyes.

"Mary, did you shoot Jake, or did Serenity?"

"When Jake went after her, I…" my voice cracked. I whispered, "All I could think about was him hurting her like he did Grace and me."

Nick's hand glided along my leg and stopped at my knee. "You had to shoot him."

"I should—" a soft sob began at what I had done. I covered my face and continued crying for the past and for now.

"You didn't have a choice," Nick murmured.

Katie cleared her throat. "I need to ask a question. Are you having an affair with Nick?"

"How dare you?" Nick snapped.

"No," I replied. "Nick and I broke up a decade ago. I work for him part-time at the tree farm as a housekeeper and whatever else is needed."

"Why'd you fire the gun? After you shot Jake, we arrived less than five minutes later. You had stalled him for ten to fifteen minutes, and then you shot him?" Katie leaned forward, arms resting across the tops of her legs. She stared. "Or did your daughter shoot him, and you're covering for her?"

"I shot him because I thought he was going to hurt Serenity."

"Maybe you shot him so you could get back together with Nick."

I lurched from my seat. "Are you accusing me of trying to *murder* Jake? Why'd you tell me it seemed like self-defense?"

"We still have to investigate, and that means all angles."

"Katie, you need to leave now. If you have more questions, we won't be speaking to you unless we have a lawyer," Nick said in an icy tone.

"We? Are you claiming you and Mary are a couple now?"

"That's not what I meant, and you know it."

"Stop it. Nick's right, it's time for you to leave." I narrowed my eyes at her.

Katie rose. "I assume you can be contacted at the tree farm?"

"Yeah, for a few days until Grace's house is cleaned." I responded, my back facing her. Without waiting for her response, I started for the receptionist's desk. Katie's accusations were like Jake's. I would never cheat on my husband, despite still caring for Nick.

The receptionist took a swig of her energy drink, the can clinking against her desk. She glanced from the computer screen. "Can I help you?"

"I'm wondering if there's any news about my husband, Jake Edwards?"

"Someone will give you a report soon." She squinted at her computer screen. "It's been… nearly three hours since the paramedics brought him into the ER."

"The last I heard, he was in surgery, and that was two hours ago."

The woman shrugged. "I don't know anything else."

A male doctor approached the desk. "You here for Jake Edwards?"

"I'm his wife."

"He's out of surgery for now. We had to resuscitate him, so he isn't out of the woods."

"Is that because of the bullet?"

"Is Jake an alcoholic? During the surgery I noticed cirrhosis of the liver, among other things."

I averted his questioning gaze and focused on Nick. Was the doctor saying Jake's drinking harmed him more than the bullet wound? After a few seconds passed, I answered the doctor.

"Look, you might as well go home. We'll call if there's any change."

Noel entered the waiting room, his hazel eyes stopping upon me. He gave a single nod and greeted Nick.

"You don't know Jake's chances?"

"I'm not one who likes to guess. It seems like you have two men waiting for you by the door, and one might be Santa." The doctor winked. "Get some sleep."

"Thanks."

I shuffled toward where Noel and Nick waited. It seemed like days had passed instead of mere hours. Jake clung between life and death. I hated the not knowing of how to feel if he lived or died.

Twenty-Five

Shrieks and woofs carried in the hallway. Sadness filled my eyes while happiness made my lips curl into a smile at the joyous sound. I wasn't sure what I felt. Jake remained between life and death.

"Wake up. It's Chwistmas," Serenity shouted, followed by a bark from Ford.

Tears slid down my cheeks and onto the pillow. Would Serenity remember that I shot her daddy on Christmas Eve? All he had wanted was his family. Footsteps dashed across my bedroom floor.

Serenity bounced on the bed. "Mommy, Mommy, Mommy. Wake up. Santa came."

A tongue licked my face in one swipe.

"Ford." I laughed and scratched his ears. "You like Christmas morning as much as Serenity does."

Someone tapped along the walls. Fingertips wrapped around the doorframe, and Nick appeared. "I think Santa Claus stole my dog."

Serenity giggled.

"Maybe Santa mistook him for a reindeer?" Nick placed his hands on his waist and exhibited a serious expression.

Ford nudged him.

"Ahh, there he is." Nick stroked the golden retriever's head. "Perhaps the thief is an elf. You seen an elf around here?"

Serenity covered her mouth, still giggling.

"No-o-o… but there's a little girl on my bed though."

"Can elves be little girls?" he teased.

Serenity scrambled off the bed and hugged Nick's legs. She lifted her chin and spoke. "I don't wanna move to the North Pole."

Nick ruffled her hair. "Should we go see what Santa's elves made for us?"

Their interaction made a lump swell in my throat. Nick would have been an excellent father to our son, had he lived. My heart squeezed at the 'could-have-beens.' The past was done. Serenity and the others were my family and my future. Whether Jake lived or died, I was done.

Breakfast aromas wafted into my bedroom and made their presence known. Brewed coffee, bacon, and pancake fragrances fought with one another for dominance. Everyone's, including Ford's, noses twitched.

"Pancakes," Serenity exclaimed. Her eyes bugged out and her mouth formed an "O".

Nick replied "Noel and Grace are making breakfast. Why don't you take Ford and go help them?"

"I love you."

Nick's face contorted. "I love—" He stifled a crack. "I love you, too, Kiddo."

Serenity and Ford took off running.

Nick tilted an ear toward the hallway and straightened forward. He shuffled with a raised forearm. When Nick reached the edge of the bed, he patted the surface before sitting. A smile broke through his pressed lips. "Grandma Hazel lives on through that girl."

"Yeah, she does. Sometimes I wonder if she came back reincarnated as my daughter."

His smile turned somber. "I'm sorry about Jake. How you feelin' today?"

I shrugged. Nick couldn't see it, and I spoke to make up for the mishap. "I… I'm… not sure."

"Mary, you had no choice. It was you or him."

"I'm so tired of killing people," I whispered.

Nick embraced me and pressed his cheek against my hair. His voice softened. "You didn't kill anyone. You defended your life, your daughter's life, and Grace's life. Jake had his demons, and they weren't gonna stop until he had killed every one of you."

"But I killed my parents, and I killed our son." Sobs wracked my body. I tightened my hold on Nick. "And if Jake dies, I killed him too."

"No, you didn't. It was their time, even if we can't understand why God took our baby boy."

"I-I-I thought being with Jake was my punishment."

"You have nothing to be punished for. I think you and I punished ourselves enough since Casper died." Nick licked his lips. "How about we stop and start fresh today?"

I wiped my tears. "Let's visit his grave today. He doesn't deserve to be alone on Christmas Day."

"I haven't been back since…"

"Neither have I."

Nick interlaced his fingers with mine. "After breakfast and presents, we can go."

"I want Noel, Grace, and Serenity to come too. We can share Casper's story with them."

"I'd like that. It's been a long time since I've been a part of a family." Nick sniffled. "I'd forgotten what it's like."

"Mommy and Nick, it's time for bweakfast," Serenity yelled.

Nick and I chuckled at her shrill voice. I asked, "Do… do you think Jake will make it?"

"I'm not sure, except he was killing himself slowly with the drinking. If Jake lives, the question is, will he keep drinking?"

"He'd have to go to a treatment center."

Serenity hollered for us again.

"Wait and see what happens. We better go join the others because it sounds like someone is eager to celebrate Christmas." Nick's lips curved into a smile, one that suggested a knowing secret.

Ford chased after a paper wad that Nick had squashed and pounced on the wrapping paper pile, causing the loose paper to scatter. Such simple things made a dog happy. I wished life was more like that.

Serenity played with a dollhouse and its accessories near the tree. Grace, Nick, and Noel had spoiled her. I examined the wooden dollhouse and dwelled back and forth on whether someone had made it. The craftsmanship reminded me of Nick's woodworking days.

Ford pawed at something under the tree. When he didn't get it, he barked.

Serenity turned. "What?"

Ford whined.

Serenity lay on her stomach and stretched for the mysterious object Ford had found. A small square box appeared. She brought it over to the couch. "Who is it for, Mommy?"

My name was written on the tag, but there was no name claiming who the present was from. "It's for me."

"Open it." Serenity shoved the box into my hands.

I slit the tape and freed the shiny wrapping paper, revealing a white jewelry box. Inside was a silver necklace. Two slender rectangular tags containing my children's names in block letters hung from the chain. My eyes moistened. I traced both of their names. "Who did this?"

"What'd you get?" Nick asked.

Neither Grace nor Noel responded.

I slipped the necklace to Nick. He felt the chain and moved to where the tags were. "Noel, was it you?"

"It was Christmas magic." Noel winked.

Serenity leaned, studying the necklace as Nick unfastened the clasp. "I'll help you put on your necklace."

I scooted closer. While I held my hair, Nick brushed the chain along my neck and fastened the clasp. "Thank you," I said.

"Mommy, what are they?" Serenity asked, staring at the tags.

"They're nametags, honey." I showed her one. "This has your name on it."

Then I displayed the other. "This says Casper. He was your brother."

Serenity's eyes widened. "I'm going to have a bwother?"

"No, he was your big brother. A long time ago before you were born, Mommy and Nick had a baby."

"Where is he?" Serenity glanced at Nick and then stopped on me.

"He died. Do you remember when you couldn't wake me up?"

Serenity nodded.

"Your brother went to sleep and never woke up."

She gave a quiet gasp. "Why?"

"No one knows. Would you like to visit him at the cemetery?" I met Noel and Grace's gaze. "We'd like both of you to come, if that's all right with you?"

"I go get dressed. Come on, Ford." Serenity darted up the stairs with her sidekick trailing behind.

"We'd be honored," Grace replied as she blotted at her stray tears.

"Mary and I were talking earlier. You two have become like family to us and, for that, I'm thankful. You're like what Christian's wife said, 'You heal what's broken,'" Nick said.

"Thank you." My voice dropped to a whisper. "For helping me and my daughter."

"Oh, honey. You're a survivor like the rest of us, and I hope you remember that when you're struggling," Grace embraced me and kissed my cheek. "You and that darling daughter of yours have become my family."

Noel rose. "I know what it's like to blame yourself. It wasn't until I started Reed's Homeless Shelter for Veterans that I learned we aren't alone in our mistakes, and that if we lean on one another, the blaming yourself lessens."

The stairs thudded as Serenity jumped each one. When Serenity reached the bottom, she padded to the closet and waited.

We disbursed everyone's jackets and their winter gear and headed outside to Grace's car.

"Are you Santa Claus?" Serenity asked Noel, who wore a red coat and Santa hat.

Noel kneeled. A peppermint stick emerged from his coat pocket, and he gave a wink. "Don't tell anyone," he whispered.

As Grace drove us, I clung to my necklace's tags. It had been a decade since I saw Casper's grave. In those ten years, I blamed myself for his sudden death and punished myself by loving an abusive man.

I reflected on Nick's statement. He was right. It was time to stop blaming myself for things that were in God's control.

Noel and Grace chattered in the front seats while Nick and Serenity did the same. I smiled. With their support, I would get through whatever happened to Jake. This was the Christmas I had unwrapped a family.

The End

If you enjoyed reading Surviving Her Christmas Present, please consider leaving a review.

To follow my author journey, please consider following me on Facebook at https://www.facebook.com/authorkyleighmccloud or by visiting my website at www.kyleighmccloud.com

Acknowledgments

I would like to thank my friend, Isabelle, for helping me find the strength to finish writing about a tough topic. Also, I would like to thank my beta readers for providing feedback.